VIA Folios 78

THE PORTABLE LENTRICCHIA

The Portable Lentricchia

Edited, with an Introduction, by

Jeff Jackson

Bordighera Press

Library of Congress Control Number: 2012936113

Printed in the United States.

Published by
BORDIGHERA PRESS
John D. Calandra Italian American Institute
25 W. 43rd Street, 17th Floor
New York, NY 10036

VIA Folios 78
ISBN 978–1–59954–040–5

for Stanislao G. Pugliese

Frank Lentricchia's Fiction

Johnny Critelli (1996)

The Knifemen (1996)

The Music of the Inferno (1999)

Lucchesi and The Whale (2001)

The Book of Ruth (2005)

The Italian Actress (2010)

The Sadness of Antonioni (2011)

The Accidental Pallbearer (2013)

THE PORTABLE LENTRICCHIA

Table of Contents

Introduction 11

1 ◆ The Mystery of Locale 25

2 ◆ Imagining the Mother............................... 33

3 ◆ The Shapes of Darkness............................ 43

4 ◆ A Life in Art.. 71

5 ◆ The Rookie Professor 83

6 ◆ Desiring Claudia Cardinale 101

7 ◆ Shooting Saddam.................................... 115

8 ◆ Two Codas 151

Appendix ◆ Writing Fiction as an Italian-American? 157

INTRODUCTION

FRANK, IN FRAGMENTS
OR: WAYS TO READ THIS BOOK

by Jeff Jackson

ONE: INTRODUCING FRANK LENTRICCHIA
In a better world, no introduction would be necessary to the fiction of Frank Lentricchia. His eight novels — which range from gentle memory pieces to brutal portraits of artists, from sophisticated meditations on time to gripping crime stories — would be required reading for anyone who fancies themselves hip to the most significant literary trends. They'd be currency. Although his books have been acclaimed by such luminaries as Don DeLillo and Gordon Lish, Lentricchia remains one of the best kept secrets in contemporary American fiction. It drives his admirers crazy. They've assembled an entire volume of criticism dedicated to exploring his novels. And now this very collection that you hold in your hands.

TWO: A SAMPLER
The Portable Lentricchia offers a substantive sampling of each of his novels to date. His books vary significantly in style and subject matter, so these selections are served like a buffet for curious readers who aren't ready to commit to a single course. The anthology's title is a nod to the famous William Faulkner primer, offered with a wink but not an apology. Taken as a whole, Lentricchia's fiction also projects the image of its own specific world. Between these covers, you'll encounter a definite sense of place, recognizable types of characters, and the distinctive sounds of their voices.

THREE: ORGANIZING PRINCIPLES
The anthology has been creatively assembled by the author. The vibrant excerpts aren't organized by novel, but according to larger thematic preoccupations: "The Mystery of Locale," "A Life in Art," "The Shapes of Darkness." Chronology often has been ignored in favor of evocative set pieces that pull on certain threads stitched throughout the entire career. "The Shapes of Darkness" places material from two early novels alongside Lentricchia's most recent effort *The Accidental Pallbearer*. Despite vastly different plots, these

passages share commonalities of tone in their eerie and unflinching exploration of violence. There's also a playful aspect to the anthology's organization in humorous-but-accurately titled sections such as "Desiring Claudia Cardinale" and "Shooting Saddam." The author has carefully carved out each of these excerpts so they stand on their own. You're free to skip around the book with a clean conscience, diving into the sections that seem most immediately appealing. However, the anthology has also been designed to be read profitably from start to finish. There's a subtle arc — climaxing in Iraq — that traces the recurring obsessions which have driven Frank Lentricchia throughout his career.

FOUR: THE ACADEMY

Which might beg the question: Which career? Lentricchia initially made his reputation as a critic and was famously dubbed "the Dirty Harry of literary criticism" by *The Village Voice*. When he turned his back on criticism to dedicate himself to fiction, the move was met with suspicion and hostility within both the academy and the reviewing community. Didn't this guy know his place? Many critics assumed Lentricchia was moonlighting and virtually ignored *Johnny Critelli*'s warm evocation of childhood, *The Music of the Inferno*'s penetrating investigation of ethnic identity, and *The Book of Ruth*'s provocative political intrigues. I suspect it wasn't the transgression of crossing the divide between critic and artist that bothered these people so much as the ease with which he successfully switched sides.

FIVE: AUTOBIOGRAPHY

Authors usually write their novels then cap off their careers with an autobiography. But with Lentricchia, it was the other way round: The autobiography birthed the fiction. Although no excerpts from *The Edge of Night* appear here, its ghostly presence can be felt throughout these pages. That book was his first leap away from being a literary critic and chronicles actual experiences in Ireland, New York City, and a Trappist monastery in South Carolina. But despite being subtitled "A Confession" and laying bare certain family narratives and fraught emotional states, this is hardly a typical memoir. It's layered with fantasies, speculations, incantatory passages that transform mundane scenes into operatic arias. The author tries on various modes and masks for size. This is autobiography as performance.

THE AUTHOR SPEAKS:
In The Edge of Night, *there were a number of characters that came into the book under their real names. They were real people and* The Edge of Night *was an autobiographical book. I did not invent those people, of course, but I imagined them. They were figures of my imagination. To what extent those imagined figures in the memoir match up to the real people of the same name is another matter.*

SIX: IMAGINATIVE QUALITIES OF ACTUAL PEOPLE

Several real people also sparked Lentricchia's first fiction, *Johnny Critelli*. This anthology opens with scenes from that novella: A reminiscence of young Lefty Lentricchia helping his grandmother pick greens for dandelion salad, a decisive little league baseball game, and a scandalous family legend involving the novel's title character. These beautifully wrought and intensely lyrical passages touch on themes that echo throughout the rest of his work. And while it's obvious here and in the following selection where the author imagines his mother that we're rooted in autobiography, it's also clear we've broken free of the confines of the merely factual. Imagine *Johnny Critelli* as a sculpture: It's chiseled from the raw material of the author's life, but the final shape that emerges is pure art, a distilled and refined fiction.

THE AUTHOR SPEAKS:
After the second page of Johnny Critelli, *I realized that my relatives were figures in a novel. They were characters and I was going to take them wherever my imagination chose to go. The inspirational power of the real people was so great that I thought it would be a dishonor not to let them have their real names. It was a way of paying homage to these people. We all know that writers derive their inspiration from real sources. We also know that writers seem to think it's important to make up fictional names for their characters, as if the creation of fiction depended on making up a name. The name is irrelevant — it's the imagining of the real, that's the relevant thing. I think that making up the name sometimes obscures the intimate relationship that the imagination has to real life. And that relationship should be acknowledged and honored.*

SEVEN: UTICA

The novels may have been initially inspired by people from Lentricchia's real life, but his fiction is most deeply rooted in place. Or as the first chapter heading has it: "The Mystery of Locale." Specifically, this mystery revolves around the Italian-American section of Utica, New York. More specifically, Mary Street in East Utica. Most specifically, the block where he grew up in 1303 and 1311 Mary Street. That block has provided the most fecund soil for his imagination. Place is the true autobiography. It's no accident that Lentricchia selected the epigrams about Mary Street to start this anthology and concludes with a moving elegy for a community that no longer exists. Nor is it any surprise that one of the key tools in his artistic arsenal is a collection of Utica city directories that he purchased from a rare book dealer and which contains the names and house numbers of the inhabitants of Mary Street throughout the years. For Lentricchia, locale and writing are inextricably interrelated. I have a theory that every book has a secret title that reveals its true contents better than the one printed on its cover. *Mary Street* is the secret title of this one.

EIGHT: ETHNICITY

But while place is an essential element of his work, some critics have mistakenly classified Lentricchia as an Italian-American writer. This may be a well meaning taxonomy, but ultimately it's misleading and reductive, neutering the work's reach and its best qualities. You don't need to hail from an Italian neighborhood to appreciate these novels — just as you don't need to be intimately familiar with Mississippi or Columbia to appreciate the fiction of Faulkner or Garcia Marquez. Lentricchia's Utica contains an entire universe. His ethnic background may initially fire his imagination, but he exhumes choice cultural details in order to explore and explode greater universal truths. These novels are among other things authentic expressions of Italian-American culture, but let's leave the cultural theorists and sociologists to pick over the bones of the topic of ethnicity. What matters here is that Lentricchia's novels are authentic acts of the imagination. In literature, this is the only authenticity that counts.

NINE: RACE

It's an instructive irony that Lentricchia has written his Utica-inspired novels while living in the South. As a longtime professor at Duke University and a resident of North Carolina, his southern experiences have filtered into his work in fugitive ways. The most important has been the theme of race, which takes center stage with his third novel, *The Music of the Inferno,* and the mystery centering around the ambiguous ethnic heritage of Robert Tagliaferro. Starting with this book, African-American characters step onto center stage, playing key roles in almost all of Lentricchia's novels.

THE AUTHOR SPEAKS:

In the famously so-called liberal North, one can live all one's life without having intimate contacts with black people. That's just the way it is. But here, for 26 years now, I've had daily contact with African Americans. In particular, this happens for me at Duke. Not only on the faculty but on the administrative staff and on the serving staff at the cafeterias. I go to the same cafeteria all the time and these women and men have been there a long time. I've formed friendships with them. We talk and they know me. We ask after each other's families. I've heard voices and vocal rhythms — which are not Caucasian voices and rhythms. We're different and the difference is wonderful! I've been inspired in that way to create characters that come directly from this experience.

TEN: CONTINUITY

Throughout Lentricchia's career, his novels have grown out of one another. The seeds of each new work are planted in the previous effort. Sometimes the novels are deeper explorations on the themes of the preceding book and other times they're born out of a powerful negative impulse, a desire to create something in direct opposition to what came before. In his first two novels, the theme of memory carries through from *Johnny Critelli* into *The Knifemen,* but each book treats them as radically different propositions. *Critelli*'s reveries of the past are ultimately healing and transcendent. *The Knifemen* views memory as an eviscerating force that deepens already unstaunchable wounds. Stylistically, *The Knifemen* is as brutally blunt as *Critelli* is unabashedly lyrical. These two short novels were initially packaged together, which probably served to confuse readers rather than make the case for the author's virtuosic range. *The Music of Inferno* followed on the heels of *The Knifemen,* delving further into its themes of memory and fathers and sons. But this time remembrance is no longer capable of containing the story Lentricchia wants to tell. A larger canvas is needed: History. *Inferno* is a Joycean evocation of time and place that's both harrowing and howlingly funny, an ambitious and symphonically structured novel that weaves the history of Utica into the very fabric of its story.

ELEVEN: RECURRING CHARACTERS

Some of Lentricchia's novels don't merely echo themes, they repeat the main characters. Thomas Lucchesi, the commercially untouchable writer of fiction, first appears in *Lucchesi and The Whale,* a playful book whose short and surreal episodes evoke Italo Calvino's *Mr. Palomar.* Lentricchia may have been drawing on his own sense of neglect from readers and critics when he created Lucchesi, but the character isn't an avatar of self-pity. Instead, he's a buoyant and often hilarious presence whose outrageous antics stamp themselves on the reader's mind. Lucchesi reappears in *The Book of Ruth,* but this time he's less a comic figure brilliantly sketched with one hand, and a more fully rounded individual as befits the more naturalistic narrative of that novel. He shares a name and some history with his previous iteration, but the reader is left with the unsettling sense that these Lucchesis are mirror images that offer different reflections.

TWELVE: CHARACTERS RECURRING

Similarly, the has-been experimental filmmaker Jack Del Piero is introduced to us as the protagonist of *The Italian Actress.* He's a largely sympathetic character who struggles to balance his relationship with a nurturing Claudia Cardinale and the Faustian pact he's offered to reignite his artistic career. He reappears in a supporting role in *The Sadness of Antonioni,* but in the few short years since his *Italian* adventures, he's been transformed from a meek washout into a diabolical bully. This startling personality shift forces readers to reassess their previous opinion of Del Piero from *The Italian Actress* and casts the themes and conclusion of that novel in a different light.

THIRTEEN: ART AS CRITICISM

Lucchesi and The Whale and *The Book of Ruth. The Italian Actress* and *The Sadness of Antonioni.* These novels each stand on their own, but when they're paired together they can be read as slippery diptychs that compliment one another. *The Book of Ruth* adds a crucial third dimension to Lucchesi's character and his artistic concerns. *The Sadness of Antonioni* is less a sequel to *The Italian Actress* than a thorough rewriting of its concerns about the seductions of art, the passage of time, and the nature of redemption. Perhaps this is where Lentricchia's previous life as a literary critic comes into play, however unconsciously. These paired novels offer more profound and vital commentaries on and critiques of each other than any critical essay. After all, literature is also criticism. Or as George Steiner says: "The best readings of art are art."

FOURTEEN: JAZZ

Lentricchia's novels don't just offer readings of each other, they also profoundly engage other texts. The early books in particular subtly weave references from other literary works into their own prose. These allusions aren't integral to the appreciation of the novels, but they forge new connections for those who notice them. In this mode, Lentricchia works like a jazz musician referencing and riffing off other works in the course of creating his own composition. This technique isn't limited to the prose; it happens with the characters as well. Starting with *The Edge of Night's* imagined encounter with T.S. Eliot, Lentricchia has incorporated various historical, artistic, and political figures into his work. *The Knifemen* prominently features O.J. Simpson. *Lucchesi and The Whale* includes both Herman Melville and Ludwig Wittgenstein. *The Book of Ruth* examines the potent trifecta of Saddam Hussein, John F. Kennedy, and Robert Kennedy. And the title character of *The Italian Actress* is none other than the iconic '60s movie star Claudia Cardinale. Lentricchia conjures these public personages not as they actually were, but as they appear to him. Or as he says: "It's the imagining of the real, that's the relevant thing."

THE AUTHOR SPEAKS:

I want to have relationships with people I can never know. Whether it's Herman Melville or Claudia Cardinale. The world is a small and narrow place for any individual. And for me the world becomes broad and more intimate and less strange if I can imagine these people in my life. This is how I can be with these people — and indeed many of them are dead. This is what I suspect is my deepest impulse — to be with these people, including the dead.

FIFTEEN: INFLUENCE

Lentricchia's early work may be steeped in literary allusions and the later work bodily haunted by writers like Melville, but his creative impulses aren't traditionally novelistic. While his novels have engaging stories, they're not mainly plot driven. His preferred mode is the lyrical and the dramatic, shot through with bursts of disruptive humor. The anthology's two codas — "The Geology of Love" and "Lament of an Escape Artist" — are ideal instances of this. Lentricchia has been energized by writers who break the rules and blaze their own paths: James Joyce, Herman Melville, William Faulkner, Don DeLillo, Thomas Bernhard. You might also detect inspiration from Harold Pinter's plays in Lentricchia's crackling dialogue, in the characters' clipped, discontinuous, and witty repartee. But although he's a renowned literary critic, Lentricchia's deepest influence isn't literary. The taproot of his sensibility and his sentences is purely musical.

THE AUTHOR SPEAKS:

The deepest influence is not a writer but a singer. I'm referring to Luciano Pavarotti. I used to go to his concerts in the 1970s when they were in smallish venues and not in arenas, when he was not an intergalactic figure. I've always been entranced by the musical style of 19th Century Italian opera and those who can bring it off. It's a style that stresses the seamless long line. The term in music is legato — a river of passionate sound and movement that has to seem endless and breathless. To me, that lies at the very heart of beauty. But you can't just have the legato effect. Frankly, it would be boring. Alongside something that has lyrical elegance, you put something staccato and abrupt and ugly. I'm very conscious of that. In revision, I try to make the differences in rhythm and tone as sharp as possible. In these changes lie the life of art.

SIXTEEN: FLUENCY

Take note of how Jack Del Piero introduces himself to the reader in *The Italian Actress*: "I'm also a periodic stutterer who would sing with all the notes connected, as in a single breath, but fluency is a river I'll not swim in: better to write than to talk."

SEVENTEEN: HER STORY

The longest section and the heart of this anthology is "Shooting Saddam" from *The Book of Ruth*. Lentricchia considers this sequence to be the best thing he's written and the most intimately connected to what he does as a writer. It features the photographer Ruth Cohen, the most prominent in a gallery of remarkable female characters in his work. Many critics, recalling that "Dirty Harry" quote, have characterized Lentricchia as a deeply male writer. It's true that he alternately embraces and undermines the machismo of Italian American culture, but this is yet another mask, one role among many. You only have to read "Imagining the Mother" from his first novel to see how adeptly he can slip into the voice and perspective of another gender. From Diane in *The Knifemen* to Claudia Cardinale in *The Italian Actress*, strong women play critical roles in his novels. And in *The Book of Ruth*, the author's supposed alter ego Lucchesi is ultimately just a sidekick. As the title makes plain, this is not his story.

EIGHTEEN: EXCERPTS

Those who've already read some of Lentricchia's work may notice these anthology selections don't always line up with their novelistic counterparts. "Shooting Saddam" and a few other excerpts have been specifically tailored to fit this collection. These sections were enmeshed in a complex web of echoes and associations that have been trimmed to focus on their most essential aspects. Most radically, the section from *The Knifemen* has been virtually remixed. The interspersed chapters involving Richard Assisi's girlfriend have been removed to create a more straightforward and headlong narrative. All these revisions have been carried out by the author himself. And as always, the reader's pleasure has been foremost in his mind.

NINETEEN: WHAT YOU'RE MISSING

But while these excerpts offer choice cuts from the work, there are many memorable passages that you're missing. The series of increasingly epic dinners in *The Music of the Inferno*. The film Jack Del Piero directs in *The Italian Actress*. The clown torture scene in *The Accidental Pallbearer*. The courtship of Hank and Jenny in *The Sadness of Antonioni*. The visionary centerpiece of *Lucchesi and The Whale* that grapples with Melville and *Moby-Dick* and transforms imaginative criticism into fiction, and vice versa. And there's much more. *The Portable Lentricchia* isn't a replacement for reading the novels, it's an enticement to engage in what Lucchesi calls "deep aesthetic immersion." There are many entry points into Lentricchia's multifarious fictional world, and hopefully this anthology inspires you to find yours.

TWENTY: IMAGINING THE AUTHOR

So who is this guy? You might fairly say Frank Lentricchia invites this question by transporting characters from so-called real life into his novels and by creating a fictional world permeated by his distinct sensibilities. It's only natural to wonder about the presence on the other side of the page. I could trot out platitudes about how he's a charismatic teacher, a generous friend, and a devoted family man. But that's not what you really want to know. Who is the writer beneath the social façade? What is the true essence of this person who's writing? Before sitting down to write his first fiction, he addressed this question in the opening pages of *The Edge of Night*. It seems appropriate for a preface to end somewhere before the work itself begins. Let's conclude with the author in the act of discovery. Let's give him the last word before he even starts to inscribe the first one.

THE AUTHOR SPEAKS:

I'll tell you what I hate about writing. Finishing it. It comes to an end. You can't come forever. When I'm finished, I can't remember what it was like inside the doing. I can't remember. When I'm not writing, I want to become a man with a brutal face.

I'll tell you what I like about writing. When I'm doing it, there's only the doing, the movement of my pen across the paper, the shaping of rhythms as I go, myself the rhythm, the surprises that jump up out of the words, from heaven, and I am doing this, and I am this doing, there is no other "I am" except for this doing across the paper, and I never existed except in this doing.

About Utica. East Utica. Mary Street. He said that Baghdad gave him the desire to write about life rooted in a place. Organic culture is how he put it. He was finally going to write his Utica novel, and do it right. Organic fiction. He'd finally cast aside the old lacerating need to write a political book. . . . He believed Baghdad would make him a political artist. But Baghdad had the opposite effect. He thought we should move back to Mary Street. He was very happy. . . .

He called himself the metaphysician of Mary Street . . . where deeds precede words and ideas. Where gestures are words. Where gestures and words cohabit, happily interdependent. Where, when there are no gestures, words are gestural — angular and lined with flesh. The voice on Mary Street is tissue, a single skin binding bodies in communication . . . listen for the grain of the voice, taste the skin of connection.

The Book of Ruth

1 ◆ THE MYSTERY OF LOCALE

EDITOR'S NOTE
Although there's a point of view switch at the end of this section, the narrator is the same throughout. In the last paragraph, he steps forward to speak from a more personal perspective.

FROM JOHNNY CRITELLI (1996)

Naturally, at the time, he was bored, and he saw nothing. Lefty? People had trouble remembering his name. It was the summer of 1956 and he was sixteen, with a red-hot driver's license, so what the heck was he doing standing around with his hands jammed down into his pockets, with her, of all people, in this public park which runs for a thousand rolling acres of great elms, and a creek where it was said that trout ran in the springtime, horribly named Starch Factory Creek. This vast green along Utica's eastern border, haven for the fifty thousand Italians of the east side. And maybe about a quarter of a mile from where he stood, perched up and sparkling on rising ground in the park's southern section, the Little League field, best in town, and site of his triumphs four years earlier, but now already passing from his memory, good riddance, already he desired deliverance from his past. Forget everything. Forget these boring Italians. This green place was most of all *their* domain. The domain especially of all these darn old Italian ladies. Hers, yes, his grandmother's, Natalina Mattia Iacovella, who just couldn't wait to make the traditional demand upon him, now that he had acquired the magical license, to take her to the park so that she could pick free dandelion salads by the bushel, all summer long grandmothers in the park bending all the way over, never kneeling, cutting into the earth, and their newly licensed grandsons so sullen and so bored peering into the future, absent. "Frankie," she had said in heavily accented English. So that must be his actual name, because that's what she said. Then in Italian: "Bring me to the park. Do this favor for me and I will make a beautiful rum cake just for you."

Naturally, thirty-seven years later, at fifty-four, he believed that he had gained sudden and inexplicable access to the past, to that very moment of his boredom in the park, standing around like a jerk with his grandmother who was picking luscious dandelions, wearing Hollywood shades (he! not the grandmother! she doesn't wear shades!), on a partially cloudy day in July of 1956, rocked back a little on his heels, wanting to be cool.

He thought he was remembering. How marvelous this hungry sweep of memory. He insisted on the word: *memory*. He loved dandelion salads. There was no limit to how much he could eat. This is what he saw, looking through the boredom: she, Natalina, a five-footer, tipping the scales at one hundred and fifty pounds, multiplied everywhere in his vision, all over the park, so many Natalinas at so many angles to his vision. Over there, just a great rounded ass. Here, frontally, massive and pendulous, the endless breasts. And such variety of side views, of the curving bodies emerged and fixed in his field of vision, out of the earth emerging and curving up and around and then back down in, where you belong, cutting in, earth-attached at the feet and hands, so many Natalinas, in a green field where she erodes a little, where she blackens in the weather.

◆ ◆ ◆

In the spring of 1952, a group of Italian-American businessmen decided to build an extraordinary Little League ball field, like a yearning for a major league stadium, in the park on Utica's east side, complete with press box and spiffy concession stands, you should have seen the dugouts: a gift to the male children of the children of the immigrants, who would play ball, go to college (first in the family to do so), and leave Utica for good. "Little League," 1952, the words were a romantic call to athletic greatness to preteen males, in this year of Mickey Mantle's sophomore season with the New York Yankees, a team whose lineup was studded with Italian-American names.

The Mick was not (apparently) Italian. He was just twenty and many of the twelve-year-old Little Leaguers on Utica's east side identified with him. "Worship" is a better word. An eight-year difference in age. What was that? They would be teammates in eight years. The Mick and me! And hadn't so many of the players' fathers already transformed him into one of us? Mantle? Who were Mickey's parents trying to kid? We knew. *Mandolino* he was called on the Italian east side. *Mickey Mandolino,* this blond bruiser from Oklahoma was actually the secret son of the great DiMaggio. He had to be, to play ball that well, to replace DiMaggio, who was the father. How do you replace the father?

Many of the males of the third generation between the Little League age limits of eight and twelve would try out, in this, the second year of Little League existence. The ball field had even been given a name: Rufus P. Cavallo Stadium.

Uniforms like the big leagues. The scoreboard, the advertisements covering the outfield fence, the smell of the hot dogs, the typewriters clicking away in the press box behind home plate, the public-address system booming out the names, you could hear it a mile away, at least. *And pitching tonight for the St. Anthony Dodgers, Lefty Lentricchia,* who had, at the time, at most, two inches on his *nonna,* Natalina Mattia Iacovella, on that night in July of 1952, when Lefty's father Frank, Frank Senior, sat in the exact middle of the bleachers between home and third base, and opposite, in the bleachers between home and first base, in the top row at the far corner, in mirrored sunglasses, a man who had been more or less on the road, working, since the summer of 1935, home now for three weeks, and drawn there to this game as much by the conflicting accounts in the sports pages as by the sport itself: *Who was this kid? Dom, Bill, Frank, Lefty, Len Lentricchia, they called him. Whose kid was he?* The man in the mirrored glasses had grown up intimately with the Lentricchia brothers, *Dom, Bill, Frank,* and then lost touch. Seventeen years ago — 1935. Whose son was this lefty hurler, who threw the ball too fast for his size and age, and whose name they kept changing? The man in the mirrored glasses was Johnny Critelli. The light that night was just right, so that you could see the image of the field reflected sharply in Johnny's glasses. You could see images of the players, his focus steady on Lefty. The eyes of Johnny C. Yourself as the image of yourself with Johnny looking right through you.

Tonight the kid was good. Faster than ever and wild enough to scare the opposing hitters. He had made one of the little tykes literally crap his pants. And even the fearsome Nick LeoGrande was tonight being held at bay. Through four innings: no hits, no runs, no walks, no errors, eight strikeouts. And even LeoGrande he had somehow struck out, but not before Big Nick had hit two balls just barely foul and so darn far that people in the stands started the scandalous rumor that LeoGrande was illegal, he was actually seventeen years old. The parents of the St. Anthony players wanted an investigation. This LeoGrande was the sweetest kid, but he was too strong for Little League. Lefty had fooled him once, but it was doubtful, they said, no, it was impossible, they said, that he could be fooled again.

There were two opinions of Johnny's looks: some said he was a handsome man; others couldn't remember, they found him nondescript. For seventeen years Johnny had been a traveling man, an extremely persuasive union organizer, who had been all over the country for so long that his tone, accent, and even rhythm had become alien. Wherever he was, people believed he was from somewhere else. Where, exactly, no one could say. Johnny Critelli was the center of many speculations, many secret images. The man's papers were not in order.

On the face of the Dodgers' pitcher, staring concentration, reflecting the father, origin of staring concentration, sitting in the third base bleachers. The father still as a statue. Tonight nothing was being given away by the faces. Except the kid's body wouldn't obey the face. With each strikeout the kid would do a little uncontrolled hop, little body spasms were taking place out there in full view of twenty-five hundred people. As if something were trying to jump up out of the body, which is what Johnny sees, too much inside, trying to jump outside. The father is perfectly stiff. Johnny believes that the kid needs to be rescued, whose ever kid he is. The help of his teammates who play flawlessly behind him will not suffice: the brilliant Tantillo will not suffice; Salerno (who consumes one hot dog between each inning) will not suffice; no, not even Tranquille, who chants rhythmically behind Lefty, *hum hum hum babe!* will suffice.

Johnny has no family, neither immediate nor distant. Only the union. Johnny has but the dimmest memory of parents. His key memories are of the brothers Lentricchia: *Frank, Bill, Dom.* And their father, *Augusto,* most of all of their formidable father. He remembers that the three brothers had three names each. Sometimes he couldn't keep them straight. He remembers the grooved intensity of their father. Whose kid was this who the papers call Len, Dom, Bill, Lefty, Frank, and, last week, Joe? Who the heck is Joe? The shortstop Tantillo is liquid smooth, floating in Johnny's glasses.

Through five innings now: no hits, no runs, no walks, no errors, nine strikeouts. One inning away from glory, baseball perfection. The Dodgers have racked up nine runs. The kid himself has hit safely twice, each time running and hopping to first base in a spasm dance. And Johnny now is beginning to react to the kid's spasms, in tiny sympathetic spasms of the shoulders, Johnny is reacting.

In the sixth and final inning Johnny Critelli feels himself urged by a cause unknown to float out and rush down upon the kid in gentle breezy force, this is the urge, to rush out of himself and soar down upon him, the boy of the spasms, and to lift him up and out, even as Lefty works hard on Big LeoGrande, one out from perfection, Johnny feeling himself leave himself, this man of ambiguous face and voice has witnessed enough of turbulence and intensity and mania, *it is time,* Johnny's hour has come round, and the kid, working hard on Big Nick, feels the floating and this is very good, this exit, this assumption, floating up from the body high above the field, this is very very good, and the father's gaze lifted up now high above the field, the father at long last drained of something too much, the father's face at long last full and sensuous, not witnessing the event unfolding right there on the field itself — the son becoming imperfect as Big Nick LeoGrande touches him harshly for the one hit that Lefty will give up that night, a high deep drive, how beautiful it is, the most beautiful thing in the world, sailing far beyond the centerfield fence: St. Anthony's 9, Ventura's Restaurant 1.

My father told me: "Johnny Critelli was for the working man. He died in a head-on collision out west, in 1952. I think it was in August. They never sent the body back. They said there was nobody to send it to." My father said: "Johnny Critelli had a terrible death."

2 ◆ IMAGINING THE MOTHER

The mother refers to the author's previous career as an academic and the books of literary theory he wrote, as well as his autobiography The Edge of Night *where she appears.*

FROM JOHNNY CRITELLI (1996)

I sit here in this spare room, in Clearwater, Florida, and I have questions on my mind. Who told my son to put our real names in a book? What am I supposed to do? Sue my own son? First he wrote nine books nobody could understand in the family, not even my nephew Tommy, who went to college. You want to know what I did with those nine books? I lined them up on top of the television. I took the pictures of his children off. I took the picture off of the first one he married whose father was a Jew. I took the second wife off who was a Lebanese. I took off my fiftieth wedding anniversary. The first two wives call me for the holidays, but my husband won't talk to them. After I talk to them he won't talk to me. Then I won't talk to him. This goes on for a couple of days. And now when we're practically in our eighties and my husband has diabetes on top of everything else my son suddenly has to write a real book that normal people might read. You know what he should do with this *Edge of Night?* Do I have to spell it out? Sideways! And if it doesn't fit up there, I'll borrow my husband's ballpeen hammer. What's wrong with an Italian girl that he never likes one? And now this new one he's with now, she claims she's Catholic. I think she's supposed to be Irish. I'm going to take a picture of this tall Irish girl. I'm going to tell her I can't put it on top of the television because there's no more room. I'll tell her even though he's my son I'm warning you, wise up fast before he puts you in a book too. He'll murder you just like everybody else. I don't talk the way he makes me talk. Does anybody? There's no more room for anybody on top of the television except himself and one nice little knickknack. Maybe he'll die first, God forbid, because if he doesn't he's going to throw our dead bodies in the city dump, then put all his television books inside the coffins instead of us. He'll ship the coffins up to Utica. He'll make them write on the stone, Buried here are my wonderful parents, my wonderful children, my wonderful wives, and if you don't believe it just dig up the coffins and look inside and you'll see my whole family who I love so much, including the wonderful Irish girlfriend, may they all be nice to one another. After he kills me in his book he expects me to love him for what he did. I'll tell you one thing. I saw his penis when he was a kid plenty of times. Naturally, I'm his mother. I was never that impressed. He'll never be the man his father was. If his father were younger he'd sweep this Irish one right off of her feet, in no time she'd go for him. I went for my husband, didn't I? Oh, my husband will defend Frank, because that's what men do, but they have no love for one another. How can they? Have you ever heard of Johnny Critelli? I heard of him once. He died a long time ago. But I never heard of his mother. He made her up. He told me on my birthday that I was based on Critelli's mother. I said to him, Who the hell is Critelli's mother? What do you mean based? He said back, She doesn't exist, Ma, that's why I based you on her. Can you understand that? Is he saying I don't exist? He claims in this *Edge of Night* that he's black! He claims he's an Italian Negro. I thank God for one thing, that I don't have to be the Irish girlfriend. I exist. I don't tell people I'm black. The Lentricchia men and their friends play cards together, they go fishing together, they watch ball games together, day and night on television. Now they even watch that goddamn golf together. How quiet they are when they watch! They have to watch constantly because they're afraid of each other. They're pathetic and I think my son finally realizes it. I got my own television now in here so to hell with them, they don't faze me. I never met the mother of the Irish one, I don't even know her name and what is she doing already who barely knows my son? She's sending my son shirts. She'll send the shirts. Then one of these days after he gets four or five shirts in the mail from UPS he'll send her one of his books for the top of the television and she'll put it up there. Because what choice does she have? Did I, the real mother, have a choice? In your eighties, which I'm almost in, you want to look at nice memories on top of your television. You want to look at a little happiness. This skinny little book he just wrote, you don't want to see that thing. *[She pauses.]* I hope he loves me. The Irish girlfriend, she's going to have to tell him she likes this book. *[She pauses.]* I better wash this bathrobe more, if you wear a bathrobe as much as I do you better wash it once a week. At least I still go to the toilet by myself. Will somebody do a person like me a favor and tell me who is my son? I think at this age I have a right to know. You lose a name here and there, you lose your mind. His book reminds me that even the good things I remember hurt me now, and this is what I see when I watch television alone in this spare room.

◆ ◆ ◆

My brother-in-law Bill called my husband moon. Hey, Moon! What a moon you got! Then he did this with his hands when he was saying those words. Have you ever seen this? This. Like this. I never saw anybody do this except Bill, my husband, and Robert De Niro. When Robert De Niro was going like this with his hands in that movie my son made us see on the VCR, he said I'm going to open up his hole. That's the kind of language my son likes, who told me he watched that movie eight times. He told me the Irish girlfriend watches it even more than he does. She's off her rocker too. They call it *Insane Bulls*. By the way, that's what Bill was. My son and his father grinned the whole time during that movie. First Robert De Niro said I'm going to open up his hole, then after that he said, I don't know whether to fight him or fuck him. What words! They stick in your mind whether you like it or not. I wonder if Robert De Niro plays tennis? Does Mickey Mantle play tennis? I think I'll ask my son who was so crazy about him. Maybe they're all queer in sports, maybe they have to be in sports, what do I know. One time Joe Fiore said something bad about Mickey Mantle when he and his wife were having coffee with us when we lived on Mary Street and my son, who was fourteen, went nuts. My son was an angel when company came over, but when Joe Fiore said that bad thing about Mickey Mantle he became vicious. We were so embarrassed. If they love a sports player watch out, it's worse than if you attack their wife. You know what Robert De Niro said to his wife? He asked her if she sucked his brother's cock off! Before that he asked his own brother if he did it to his wife! My brother-in-laws are bad, but we never went that far in this family. I never got asked a question like that. But Robert De Niro's wife I heard fools around. My husband was called moon because he was lucky in cardplaying. Bill had a lot of language. Bill was saying my husband always wins in poker because of his big moon, but my husband's moon is not that big, it's just right and I like to look at it when he doesn't know I'm looking. According to Bill, my husband's hole was very big, that's why he was lucky. That's what this means, like this, your hole is big and it's open, like this. Isn't this a nice gesture? I think I'm the first woman to ever do it, unless my son taught it to the Irish girlfriend, which I wouldn't put it past him. Unless she already knew, which I could believe that too. I could believe anything about her. I don't know her well and maybe at my age I never will, but I know one thing about her. My son better stay in line because she'll open up his hole without thinking twice. I shouldn't say this because he's my son, but in my opinion it's about time a woman opened up his hole once in a while. When you do that to them once in a while they're easier to get along with and then after a while they like it, you have to shit on them once in a while, which they like even when they say they hate it. They like a lot of things they won't admit. We make them do things and they like everything we make them do. Can you figure any of this out? What the heck does luck have to do with your moon having a nice big hole? The only thing I can figure out is Bill was constipated a lot, which is true. He thought it was lucky to go easy every day, which is true about my husband, and which is definitely lucky. In other words, Bill was jealous about what went on inside my husband's beautiful moon. In that department my husband never had a problem in his life. I agree with Bill because I have that problem myself constantly. My husband is so lucky, it pours out every day. No strain. There's my husband playing poker like he's sitting on the toilet at the same time, so happy like he is every morning without fail and he's winning all the pots so smooth and so easy and Bill is saying *Madon'*, Hank, what an ass on you! Thank God he didn't refer to a piece of ass, I'm confused as it is by the way they talk in the Lentricchia family. People like Bill and me, we have to strain. Bill the big talker can't go. My husband says I talk too much and maybe if I keep my mouth shut more and stop worrying about moving my bowels I'll get over my bowels problem. I told him does he want me to get over it the way Bill got over it? You know how Bill got over it? I'll tell you how. He died, that's how. He died indirectly because of this problem, screaming and completely insane, he saw himself on television eating ice cream, and I saved my husband's life indirectly because of this problem because of what happened that New Year's Eve at Bill's house where the four of us were sitting around talking and all of a sudden the subject came up of hemorrhoids, which is another thing Bill and I had in common and my husband who is so mooney never had. Hemorrhoids are not lucky but Bill would have been lucky if it was hemorrhoids, even if he had the type where they have to operate. Imagine a sharp knife up there! I was saying to Bill, when you have our condition it's a good thing to look at the toilet paper every time you wipe, it's even good to look in the bowl to see the differences in there among your stools from day to day, they tell you about your state of health, when it comes to your state of health those things tell the truth about you, including your state of mind, don't kid yourself. Bill's wife was looking at me funny. My husband was looking irritated because he doesn't appreciate this type of discussion. He says to me, Why do we have to have on New Year's Eve a medical conversation? Lately, I said (I made believe I didn't hear my husband), I was seeing a little on my toilet paper. Suddenly my brother-in-law who always listened to me very seriously said in a loud voice: A little blood on the toilet paper? You think it's bad on the toilet paper? When I go you see it in the bowl! My toilet is so full of blood sometimes I can't see what I put in there! I said, Bill, that doesn't sound right to me. You better go to the doctor because that's not hemorrhoids. My husband looks at the wall and says, Dr. Lentricchia. Bill says, Why? So they can suck me dry? They say your hemorrhoids, Preparation H, fifty-five dollars. Don't make me laugh, he says, because after a certain age it's natural to bleed from your ass. My husband says, Don't harp on him, it's his internal affairs. Bill's wife gets up to make the coffee. All of a sudden Bill took my breath away, he doubles up and starts crying the way he did when Angie Bombace wouldn't take him back. We were frozen in our chairs watching him rolling on the floor crying and hollering. His wife from the kitchen said, Dear, did you say something? Two months later he told her off good, who wasn't hard of hearing. He told her her lousy American cooking which had no taste caused the cancer, it wasn't hemorrhoids and it was all over his liver and in his mind in the end. Bill was full of cancer on New Year's Eve. My husband and I got out of our chairs. My husband was crying. Bill said, Hank, I think I'm going bye-bye. I said, Don't talk that way, Bill, we all love you, even the one in the kitchen and the ones who used to be in the kitchen. Seven months later he was dead. The following April, Eckerd's was giving out those stool tests free. I made my husband take that test. I had to harp on him but finally he did it. He said, Why? There's no blood. I said, They have machines now they can see microscopic blood in your stool. I said, When it's microscopic they can cure you. You want to end up like your brother, up in Utica, under all that snow, just because he had a hard head? I had to help him take that test, I've done it a million times. He didn't know how, you're the expert he says like a wise guy, you put your hand in there. I put my hand in. It turned out to be microscopic. They claimed they got the tumor and he lived. Good thing I harped. Now I can still look at my husband coming out of the shower. He lost his shape but so what? If that's what it takes, I'll put my hand in every day. Bill wasn't mooney, that sounds pretty snotty but it's true. The funny thing is, do you know what I remember best about Bill? Something crazy he used to do with his moon. It was something different. Years ago he was a moon artist. I don't mean what those kids do, anybody can do that, that's not an artist. Bill was an artist of the moon nobody ever heard of! He used to get a lot of gas and save it up somehow, nobody to this day knows how. Then he would go from chair to chair, first a wood chair, then a leather chair, then a cloth-covered one, then he went up against the plaster wall, against the doorknob, tight he went up against each thing with his moon, letting out a little in each place, first tight, then letting half his moon off a little bit each time because it was different material and different amounts of gas and different gaps of lifting, a different sound each place, high, low, deep and dark, how fast he ran around in our living room! and after a while it was just Bill, it was only Bill, dancing and playing his moon voice, I don't even think he knew we were there after awhile, he was going around and around, he was gone. I saw this with my own eyes, he would have done it on the ceiling, he would have arisen if he could, and this is Bill, this is an artist, and now he is gone for good and I suddenly realize either I'm remembering or I'm exaggerating like my son, Mr. Exaggeration. I'm trying to have Bill on my mind, for sure I'm trying to have Bill on my mind, and that's not an exaggeration. I admit what my husband says is true. My son and I are a lot alike. But it would break my heart if after what I just told you you came to the conclusion that Bill was odd.

I remember the light on top of the ambulance in the dark going around and around. This was in August of 1949. Then the people on our block must have all come rushing out of their houses the way they always did whenever an ambulance or a police car stopped on our block. They were standing in the driveway staring down at me. Eva the big mouth next door was the head one as usual, in her housecoat, which she was usually bare under that summer. I felt drowsy and the funny thing was, this is what I remember better than anything, I had no cares for my family. Isn't that something? They were wheeling me down the driveway in one of those stretchers with wheels on and I was on a cloud. I didn't know where my daughter was. My mother-in-law must have been taking care of her in the kitchen giving her cookies, and I have to admit that it didn't matter one way or the other where she was. My husband who was walking beside me wasn't looking at me, he was looking at the driveway in his T-shirt. I didn't want to say, Frank, look at me, I'm your wife. He had finally filled out nice, his muscles in his chest and arms were very beautiful. I don't have any idea to this day what he was going through because we never had a conversation concerning this, but I'm positive he wasn't playing tennis in his mind for a change, but who knows for sure. I heard my son's voice say somewhere in the dark what's wrong with my mother. My son Frankie was nine then, playing outside in the dark. He must have seen the light on top of the ambulance. I heard Eva say to him there was too much blood. That's all she said. There was too much blood. My husband kept looking at the driveway and walking and saying nothing. The crowd didn't talk and I couldn't see my son, who must have been in the crowd staring. I heard these things going down the driveway but I didn't belong to these things for a change. I was just going to sleep in August with all those blankets on me and that's all it was. They must have thought I was cold. I wasn't cold or hot. I wasn't anything for a change. Back then people were different with their kids. We didn't tell them I was pregnant. It was too embarrassing back then to talk like that. Besides, because of the risk we didn't want to disappoint them. I was told to stay in bed because Dr. Panzone said I might not keep it because of the spotting a little too much. That night I started to get terrible cramps and the spotting became a river. After I soaked the mattress they called an ambulance. I was just full of blood down there. Two children without trouble, now this. You know when I stopped wanting to have another one? The true answer is never. Through my fifties and sixties and even these days once in a blue moon I wish I had another one. They always say you should be grateful for what you have, but I keep thinking about the one who died inside me. I guess I became my baby's coffin, didn't I? My son was old enough to have been told about what happened, but he wasn't told until his late twenties. We didn't have the words to talk to a nine-year-old like that. My husband could have taken him with us in the ambulance, so what if I died right there? But then we would have been forced to say something to him in the ambulance. He would have seen them put that thing on my face. I don't think he needed to see that. Why didn't Eva at least lie? You don't tell a nine-year-old there's too much blood when in the dark his mother is going down a driveway into an ambulance out of the blue. I'm mad now, but I wasn't mad then. You should see my husband's face when I say I wouldn't mind having another one. I could use a cat or dog. This morning on "Donahue" I heard a woman professor say something that was very intelligent. She said what happened to me should be called a natural abortion. When she applied that word to me, I felt like slapping her face. I never had a picture of it in an album. I can't even have one in my mind. I've tried hard to make up a face in my mind. My son is so damn stubborn, I can't tell you, or I would ask him to do me a big favor. You wrote a Critelli. Now do this for me. I would like to ask my son if he has to write about us and make half of it up why can't you make me one in your mind, Frank, make me one in your mind and then put it in words in a book where I can read it every day. Make a picture of a face close up. Make it six months old, who cares whether a girl or boy, and let it be healthy, and say I nursed it until it was one year old. Knowing my son, he'll say I nursed it until it was ten. *[She pauses.]* I went to the toilet, and it fell out of me in pieces. *[She pauses.]* Write me a baby, Frank. Is that so hard to do if you're a writer?

3 ◆ The Shapes of Darkness

EDITOR'S NOTE

The opening of this section is related in third person, then the narration is taken over by Richard Assisi who works as an OB GYN. The O.J. Simpson trial takes place in the present tense of the book. The past is many years previous.

FROM THE KNIFEMEN (1996)

On the night in the spring of 1965, when he learned of his father's death, Richard Assisi slept soundly and dreamt of a child of three, or possibly four, 1943 or '44, all dressed up in the uniform of the United States Air Force. Such a brave little man was he, standing on the corner in knee pants, and with those rosy cheeks of olden times photography, wrapped tightly in a column of sunlight, and frozen in salute on a cold and rainy day in late autumn, when a rickety car pulled merrily to the curb. Toot! Toot!! Toot!!! The driver looked out at the child shyly, he smiled a little, and said: "I knew you were hungry, so I came." The child was happy now, because he was indeed hungry, he was starving, when suddenly there appeared another man, in a long coat with deep pockets, who approached the rickety old car stealthily, as the shy driver, the child's daddy, looked out at the child with such longing that he forgot himself and saw only the child and not the stealthy man standing at his door, leaning and peering in, reaching deep into his left-hand pocket, the two men in dark cold, the happy child saluting in sunlight, when with his right hand the man in the long coat returned the child's salute, while with his left he pulled from his pocket a long pistol and shot the driver through the head, blowing brains and blood everywhere. How the child clapped! And how he hopped up and down, as the stealthy man reached quickly into the merry car and stole a sandwich wrapped in bloody wax paper, then cunningly tossed it too high to the child, who leapt like Joe DiMaggio and snagged it, one-handed catch! "Bravo, American soldier boy! and hello," said the stealthy man, "I am proud to be at your service." But the child paid no attention because he was so eager to unfold the wax paper to find what he knew would be there: a luscious sandwich of little sausages and red peppers, his favorite of all good things to eat. And so he ate, quite greedily he ate, and when he finished, the man in the long coat wiped the child's bloodied mouth with his left hand and said: "Take this hand and come with me, or you'll be alone for your whole life." So the child took his hand, and off they went, as the child sang out, "Toot! Toot!! Toot!!!" merrily merrily down the street, into the cold and dark.

◆ ◆ ◆

It comes in the summer of my obsession with the tribulations of Orenthal James Simpson. June 29, 1994. After thirty-two years of silence, a call from Victor Graziadei. Victor again, the man my father once told me had no life. I said "You mean of his own?" "No," he says, "I mean no life." I say, "Like yourself?" My father ignores the snottiness. Without a trace of rancor, and almost without fail, he turns the other cheek.

My father told me he had such hope that I would stay away from Victor, as far as possible, even though it wasn't his place, he said, to say so. I have no idea what his place is. My father is blurry. Even though he knew I couldn't, he told me that I should make an effort. "Unless you need to eat yourself alive, Richard."

When the phone rings, I'm reaching into my stash of chocolate chip cookies, arranged before me on the coffee table, in geometric patterns with my reserve of Fig Newtons. Diane calls them "frigs," "your beloved frigs." Against my will, I find myself drawing ever nearer to Diane. Victor doesn't say, "Hello, this is Victor." He says, "How many hours with Orenthal today?" I reply, "Every minute, plus I taped. I thought you were dead." "No," he says, "you are." I say, "Tell me your opinion of our friend. I need to know." He says, "It looks bad for Orenthal, but she apparently did something." I say, "Of course, she's a cunt." He says, "Was. Was a cunt. And he's just a prisoner of love." I say, "We make no excuses." He says, "Orenthal and you." I say, "Orenthal and me and you, in our blood-smeared galoshes." "Ah," Victor says, "we converse." He pauses. Then he says, "I've kept track of you through Carmen, who's still alive, and who you abandoned. Notice that our man has a girlfriend of Italian background." I say, "Proves he's an asshole." Victor replies, "The meaning of this woman is that we have long been associated with affairs that enrapture this nation." I tell Victor, "Your stories about our ethnic background always confused me." He says, "You desired involvement in the moods I was attempting to project. Don't kid yourself. Orenthal sandpapers his skin. And who can blame him with a name like that? He sucks on it. Behind the scenes, he sucks on it hard." I say, "Behind the scenes of his charisma and sweetness." "Yes," Victor says. "Rage like candy. Which reminds me. It dawns on me you're in love again. True or false?" I say, "Definitely. This time I'm going to extract satisfaction."

Toward the end of the conversation, I tell Victor that my air conditioner has broken down, "in this debilitating humidity." He says, "Good. You will embark upon a course. According to Carmen, you became the Chief Finger-Fucker. True or false?" I reply, "That's a way to put it." "Richard," he says, "tell me something. Is it possible for people of Italian background to eat properly where you live? Is the cannoli as we have always understood it, up here, possible in the Land of Cotton?" I say, "In exile, we suffer." A long silence. Then he says, "Someone created a spectacle in Los Angeles. Someone could have been somebody in my business, which you weren't. Tell me, Richard, hath fresh semen been descried in her vagina, and in her anus too? Was the loveliest of all our lassies gutted, skinned, and quartered?" He laughs. He says, "Happy Birthday!" He hangs up.

I'll try harder to stop talking about my father in the present tense.

It was the early fall of 1959, my first semester at Oneida County College, and I came into Carmen Caravaggio's Italian Pastries and Coffee Shop, corner of Bleecker and Mohawk, bearing my brown valise full of books, heavy enough to give me a hernia. Empty, except for Victor Graziadei and Carmen himself. Victor says, loud enough for me to hear, "I've been onto that kid from the start." Victor's voice is a deep hot bath. Carmen says, "Get over here, big fella, I have to introduce you to your destiny." I was a regular at Carmen's, but I had never seen Victor in there. In fact, I had never seen Victor in a stationary position. Carmen was eight years my senior, he was my next-door neighbor on Mary Street, and he was about to introduce me to a man who lived all his life across the street from us, and just a short block farther east. The cross street of Wetmore between us. Mary runs parallel to, and one block south of, Bleecker, Utica's Italian-American main drag, which Victor, who didn't own or drive a car, wore out, day in and day out, when he didn't take the bus at the corner of Wetmore and Bleecker. Don't worry about visualizing the tedious map. The map comes back. So does the bus. Bleecker runs west to the center of town, where it changes its name as it runs through the Polish west side. It was well known all along Bleecker that Victor, once a week, bearing a big black valise, bigger than mine, walked into Polish territory, sometimes detouring through a black neighborhood. To disappear for a few days. To perform a deed, as he told me much later.

Until that moment at Carmen's, I had never heard Victor's voice. With the exception of Carmen, I didn't know anyone who had ever talked to Victor. I didn't even know anyone who knew anyone who knew anyone.

Carmen gave me his chair. When he was out of earshot, Victor said, "The only man in Utica without malice." I said, "What?" Victor said, "We don't have a lot of time. Carmen has made an unusual success in this business. Carmen is a well of kindness. In other words, they hate him in this town." I said, "Who?" Victor said, "Forget it. They can't stomach him. We don't have a lot of time. You need to know about our first meeting, which I don't believe you recall. November 1941." I said, "In November of 1941 I was about six months old." He said, "That's one of my major points. This is not a story that leads into Pearl Harbor. I know something which you don't, which in later years may be helpful, when you wonder in your despair if you'll ever change. We are who we are. True or false?" Victor was in his late thirties. I was eighteen and a little embarrassed. He paused for a long time, his eyes still on me, mine trying to focus on the espresso. Then he said, "With men who enjoy each other's company, these awkward moments are traditional. After a point, you learn to accept the pain. You learn to love it." Victor said "men."

"Carmen," he said, "please, we need some now." Carmen came out of the backroom bearing a tray of three cannoli. Victor quickly seized two without a word. This slightly aggravated me. It slightly aggravates me even now to think about it. Victor read my mind. He said, "This is also one of my major points. You want what I have, from the beginning this is the case. Don't think I'm without the civilities. I'm attempting to dredge up a scene that lurks inside you, because you are who you are. Richard, I stand on the corner of Bleecker and Wetmore on a cold rainy day in November of '41, holding in my hand a pink cloud of cotton candy. I stand on the corner of the bus stop for those going east, but I am not waiting for the bus that goes east, because I never go east. I stand at that bus stop because on this lousy day there's a big splash of sunlight exactly there and nowhere else. I'm happy by myself in the sun. I'm eating and enjoying the beautiful leaves rotting on the sidewalk. Then a bus comes from the west. The driver thinks I'm waiting for him with my cotton candy, or maybe somebody wants to get off, regardless, and that's why he rolls to a stop. I never found out, because of what blossomed in front of me. A small boy comes flying on his bike down the little rise of Wetmore. He's flying toward me on the sidewalk. The bus is slowing to a stop, probably for me, though in retrospect I hope not. The boy puts on his brakes, like he must have done a thousand times. But this time he starts to skid on the wet leaves, and when he skids out into the sunlight he hits a section of dry sidewalk skidding too fast with his brakes on hard, and suddenly the bike flips, and over the handlebars he goes sailing in the sun in his blue jacket, the face still having fun. Richard, the face never caught up with the situation. The head makes a sound when it hits the curb. The bus is rolling to a stop while the body is sliding over the curb, and under the bus he goes, just as the bus stops, under the bus he goes, but not all the way under, which is what he needs to do. The timing couldn't have been better. He starts to go under headfirst in front of the back wheel, which rolls to a stop directly on top of the head. The head explodes. Blood all over me, including the cotton candy. First a little pool, then a stream flowing toward the curb. Flowing into the sewer. Brains, teeth, an eye. My mouth is screaming. It must have been my mouth, because it couldn't have been the siren of the ambulance yet, I had a sore throat after, and they come pouring out of their houses without their coats on before the siren, so many women, including your mother, pouring down the rise they come, including the mother and grandmother of the boy, who know before they get there. They all know before they get there. Except you. You in your mother's arms, with your face rooting relentlessly at her breast, which you're getting at through a special slit she made in her dress just for you. Richard, you were relentless. When your mother gets there, the screaming, not immediately, but pretty soon pulls you off the breast, and your head turns toward the carnage. At such a time, you could get completely out of hand, this would have been acceptable at that time, because you don't appreciate the transition, but you didn't get out of hand, because in the sunlight your eyes catch the blood and you are so fascinated by the colorfulness all before you. Your arm comes out and your hand points down at the crap. You smile, you make a sound that a parent likes to hear. Goo. Your mother, when you did that, definitely wanted to smile. Who could blame her? It wasn't you who had been destroyed on Bleecker Street, thank God it's not my son down there, with a head like a pancake, who they can't have a wake for unless they close the coffin. Then something else catches your eye. Your arm does the same thing. Then it's back and forth, with little turns of the head, between Bobby Zito's bright blood and my cotton candy. You're happy. Goo Goo Goo. Bobby Zito, who lived directly across the street from you. Like this your head, Richard. Like this. Goo Goo. Okay, Carmen, bring him another one now."

Carmen came out of the backroom with another cannoli. Carmen said, "We've been planning this for a long time. To give you perspective. Enjoy yourself, Richard." And so I enjoyed myself, because no one made a more beautiful cannoli than Carmen Caravaggio, not even my maternal grandmother, may she rest in peace.

In September of 1963, when I left Utica for good, Victor said: "Richard, may the life you take not be your own."

◆ ◆ ◆

The cookie crumbs dirty the expensive oriental carpet beneath my coffee table. You know the coffee table I mean: the one between the couch and the TV. When the commercials come on, I go, whether I have to go or not. A few drops forced out and shook off from the sitting position, the utility and comfort of which I discovered at an age much younger than you'd expect. I've eliminated the splash effect universally associated with my gender. It takes me until the third day of the preliminary hearing to discover Court TV, and constant, commercial-free coverage: Orenthal full time. No appropriate time now to go, or to vacuum the cookie crumbs, or to observe the woodchuck who has moved into my yard. "The chuckster," as my friend across town, the redoubtable Diane, refers to him. She claims the chuckster is male. She says that I should be careful when I'm in the yard. That I should keep my wits about me, and my pants buckled tight, when in the yard I bend over. Because the chuckster wishes to perpetrate. Diane's colorful phrase is, "Fuck you up the ass." My heart leaps up! This kind of humor is typical of my friend, who is no cunt. Victor is wrong. They're probably not all cunts. I could give many examples, and probably will, of her delightful wit. I thought I was going to write, "many examples of noncunts." We improve. Victor said that Yeats said, "Men improve with the years."

Victor is a distorted human being. I have come to understand this, and Carmen, kind Carmen, is not far behind, that son of a bitch. I'm changing. In recent years, I've established proper psychic distance from the corrupters of my youth. Especially Victor. Not that I'm about to relent. "Let me in." "No." "Please." "I said no." "Why?" "Don't force me into specifics. You lack discipline. Don't force me to enumerate." "Give me specifics. Something to work on, as I grieve." "Don't break my balls, Diane." She folds her arms. So I say, "Crumbs. The bedspread. These are examples of a condition hostile to my happiness. The hostile condition is you. The kitchen counters. Don't force me to pile up the evidence. The blood on the toilet seat. Happy now? The blood on the toilet seat, and not just once. I'm pretty sure it wasn't butt blood, Diane." She cocks her head. She says, "You would know the difference."

He, my chuckster, has taken to living under the house, and is responsible, I'm convinced, for the broken air conditioner. My goal is to hand-feed him. The odors rise, heavy and moist, through the humidity, through my gleaming hardwood floors, from the roly-poly little cocksucker shitting under my house, who leavens my day during the interminable recesses, when they go off as a unit to the judge's chambers, leaving me to fend for myself, perchance to pee. And then off they go to eat their elegant Los Angeles sandwiches, delivered directly to an antiseptic room without windows, in the Criminal Courts Building, prosecution and defense teams together at last, in a semi-informal setting, sharing humorous anecdotes, planning further recesses, whining that they don't have time to go off to their respective bistros.

We, on the other hand, take everything personally. He in his two-thousand-dollar suits, me in my pajamas and red robe, the latter purchased three childless marriages ago. We eat alone. We do hundreds of sit-ups. We think. Of air fresheners, for example, and not only because of what he's doing under my house. There are many odors in my house that I cannot trace to the chuckster. And he, Orenthal, in his cell, thinking of similar needs, asleep in brutalizing proximity to his toilet, praying over his toilet. By the way, when she said "as I grieve," she was laughing, I believe. I could be mistaken. She was possibly crying. Fuck her, or don't fuck her, as the case may be.

Carmen's place met the sanitary standards of the operating room, which is how the Joint Chiefs of Surgery liked to refer to it. "A surgeon," Carmen says, "someone they pay and honor to knife people. Richard, we recommend you take it up in college. Major in surgery, because we need assistance in here. The workload is out of control." He says, "The kid is involved. He's perfect. The kid is fucking hopeless." Carmen laughs so fetchingly.

A day after our first meeting, I'm walking down Wetmore to the bus stop on the corner of Bleecker (to go west), Victor coming to me from the opposite direction. He starts talking when he's still fifteen feet away: "I understand through Carmen that already at your age you're involved in homicidal frustration. Carmen has seen you comport yourself with your father's car in a crazed manner. Carmen claims that humiliation in your high school period was constant. The skinniness, you're a string bean, Richard, the pimples, the ridiculous hair, etcetera. You tend to present yourself in a queerish manner. Boils in unlikely places. Carmen claims one in your anus. How does Carmen know? Most of all, the valise, Richard. In high school, with the roughnecks you went to high school with, a tender boy with a valise is an obvious asshole, which you were conscious of, you were a target, and yet you insisted on the valise, which convinces me you're well suited. Oh yes, you tower over me, and in your presence I verge on shyness and rage. You for your part are unusually sensitive concerning my forearms. You hunger for masculinity of the forearm. Look at my wrists, Richard. The thickness, behold the thickness and seethe. You're invited to my home tonight at eight. Honor me at eight, and leave your sullen face at home, because I'm not your father." These last words spoken as he walked away.

To this day, I consider it a sign of my normality that I listened to him without response; that I was scared; that I was eager for eight o'clock. I couldn't wait any longer. I wanted a girlfriend. I wanted to lash out. I wanted Victor to act as nuts as he talked. I wanted a physique. I wanted to attach my ugliness to his secret extremity, whatever his secret was, in secret consummation, no more masturbation, no more of that. I wanted to say to Victor: "We've had this date from the beginning."

In 1959, what I am is a six-one, 145-pound, dirty blond, the King of Acne, with glasses. Not that Victor was himself an amazing specimen, Utica's own Cary Grant he wasn't — though, speaking of Cary, there were these odd moments when I thought I could detect the faintest trace of a cultured English accent. When he said the word "humiliation," for example, or "cunt," especially "cunt." Victor with all that wiry carrot-colored hair, the paleness of the face, 170 pounds, five seven, no fat. The shocking carrot-top, unvalidated by genealogy or chemicals, is subject to tedious rumors. Victor Graziadei: president and sole proprietor of Utica Meat, Inc., a slaughterhouse.

When Carmen, Victor, and I occupied the pastry shop by ourselves, it was the House of Freaks, and Carmen's classic Southern Italian aspect only enhanced the effect. The thick black hair, the swarthiness, the ample pouty mouth. Carmen is all passivity and enervation, despite his frenzied application to the business. Sloe-eyed Carmen, at five six, he oozes it, with just a hint of a fifties sweater girl, giving one considerable difficulty, so it was widely stated back then, whether one should fight him or fuck him. Even then, in spite of my vague reservations, my vaguer discomfort, I drew near to Carmen.

My father said he was a generous man, yet to be feared. So many times he had given me a box of his beautiful pastries to take home to my father. I said, "Generous, like you." My father said nothing. I said, "To be feared. Not like you in the least." He said, "Richard, stop stoning me with that song. Your mother had no qualms." "Meaning what?" I said. "That you didn't nauseate her?"

Carmen's place: I see it still. White ceramic floor tiles, framed in black grouting. Wrought-iron tables and chairs. The short back wall, brilliantly black-lacquered behind the stainless steel showcases. The long cool side walls in soft gray, accented by six huge black-and-white photos of Naples: street urchins, both sexes, various stages of undress. You could lick your gelato off the floor. Someone did. Someone had to. Glass of the showcases, cleaned thrice daily by Carmen himself, and no one else, with a vinegar-and-water solution.

One time, when it was just Carmen and me at the shop, Utica's Princeton-educated mayor, J. Kenneth Sherman, asked Carmen in the Princeton manner why he hadn't "worked more Italian colorfulness into the decorative scheme, you know, the Italian gaiety, Carmen." Carmen replied, "Your Honor appreciates Richard's perfect ass, doesn't he?" Mayor Sherman hugged himself. Carmen Caravaggio knew about the boil in my anus because I told him about it.

At a minute and a half before eight, I leave home for Victor's, proceeding along the north, or poorer side of Mary Street, side of narrow two-family houses, then cross, at the appropriate point, to the south side of wide and much better kept two- and three-family structures, with porches on all floors sweeping along importantly across the entire front face. What I know, at this moment, as I'm about to knock for the first time on Victor's front door, is that Victor lives alone, in the home willed to him, only child, by parents who looked like Carmen's type of Italian. I know also that they willed him Utica Meat, Inc., where Victor rarely appears during business hours, preferring, according to persistent rumor, to work on the books starting around midnight, departing just before dawn.

Victor, as always, freshly scrubbed and freshly clothed, opens the door as I climb the steps. No greeting. We skirt the edges of the living room in order to avoid the leaning stacks of newspapers, magazines, and official-looking documents, and the sea of used envelopes, grocery bags, unopened personal mail and old bills, and the piles (neat, twine-bound) of what look to be manuscript pages of poems. Ancient heavy furniture, badly frayed rugs, walls darkish with strange stains. Several days' worth of unwashed dishes still in the dining room, leather-bound volumes of the master English and American poets strewn everywhere on the floor. Above all: the stench. I follow him to the back foyer, where we ascend the stairs to the second-floor apartment. As he opens the door, he says his first words. "But in here we resist," and the door gives upon an apartment fragrant with disinfectant: burnished hardwood floors, freshly painted white walls, ceiling removed, partitions knocked out, all space vaulting to the roof. A loft effect. Barren. Except at the dead center (Victor once called it "the death center"), a small unfinished wooden table: lamp, inkstand, legal-sized pad, black quill, sharp-edged wooden chair. On the floor, front of table, stacked in three neat rows, what looks to be a full *Encyclopaedia Britannica*. Victor says the letter *M* is missing, because "this is where I'm up to. It's in there," and he points to what I take to be a bedroom, but the door is closed. Victor says, "We'll never go in there. The letter *M*, for murder. Richard, I want to introduce you to Utica Meat, it would delight me. Plus Carmen tells me you need a part-time job to tide you over what the scholarship doesn't cover." I say, "In this town, to get part-time work you need pull. My good father has no pull." Victor says, "That's because your good father is good. But now you know somebody who is not good. I require a shackler between eight and midnight, weekends only. Let's take a walk and I'll show you the place. This," he says, indicating the ascetic space with arms outspread, "this is me." Arms still outspread. "When you're a little older, knock on wood, you'll have this too." Arms down. "Then you'll be me." He grins. "True or false, Richard?" I say, "Victor, I need to attempt to say something serious." He says, "With me you can feel free." I begin to weep heavily. My head on his shoulder. Victor is silent. I finish weeping. I've said nothing. He says, "I appreciate the confidence you show in me, Richard. Now let's go down to the slaughterhouse. I'll bet a kid like you doesn't even know what a shackler is. True or false?" I say, "True." He says, "Never mind. You'll love it."

◆ ◆ ◆

It's located several blocks north of Bleecker, in the old industrial district, on a badly lit east-west thoroughfare of rough-house saloons, broken beer bottles, and occasional condoms, sagging with semen, from chain-link fences hung with care. I walk this street for thirty minutes in the dark, glancing frequently over my shoulder at Victor trailing some distance behind. "No offense," he says at the outset, "but I don't want people to think that in my late thirties fraternization is welcome." Suddenly, rounding a sharp bend, at last the slaughterhouse, a vast cinder-block affair. Atop four high poles, massive electrical fixtures — worthy of a small outdoor stadium — bathe the place and its adjoining areas in harsh light. Clustered all along one side, an array of covered holding pens; jutting far out from the other, the loading dock, where trucks a mile long take on hundreds of frozen carcasses for the trip to New York, and where the small, shabby trucks of obscure local entrepreneurs haul off profitable barrels of yesterday's guts, hooves, hides, and heads. Above the main entrance, surprisingly small, in red neon:

UTICA MEAT INC.
SINCE 1938
GRAZIADEI

"Everything here we use for something," Victor says, "except the blood, which is good in itself, like the fine arts of mankind. We just stare at it. You start with the fine arts, Richard, eventually you have a progression direct to blood, and vice versa. Which they don't teach in college. Don't forget the vice versa, and don't contradict me, because you know I'm right."

As we walk through the front gate, we're greeted by a scream, apparently from within, a sound of shattering size sustained on the night air, arching up and out over the city, then yielding, as if by virtuoso technique, to seamless diminuendo. Then nothing. Victor is saying, "The fat lady can sing," and he's ushering me past the loading dock, toward the back of the place, and I'm needing to assume an animal origin, saying, "What was that?" And he, dead-pan, "*Or who was that?* All these years, Richard, I'm still not used to it, thank God. Are you thrilled?" At the back, a flight of exterior stairs leads to a tiny door just under the roof. We stoop through single file into an opaquely en-closed catwalk ending at another door, this one opening into Victor's glass-enclosed office, hanging high above the center of it all: a commanding view of the killing floor and the swing shift going full blast.

I think Victor wanted me to be seduced by what I saw. I think he wanted me to live in another world, his world, and I was eager. The two of us just standing there in his office, surveying the colorful scene beneath us, and then, after a long while, Victor says, "You're struggling not to smile, think I don't know? You're trying to keep your arm at your side, because you don't want to point. Your mind is remembering against your will. But let's face it, Richard, you're too mature now to say Goo, Mommy! Come on, Riccardo, let's go downstairs. Let's get involved. Later on, we'll go across the street and see Uncle Henry, who I believe you've never met." Victor was referring to the only family dwelling within blocks, a Victorian three-story structure, exceptionally maintained: Uncle Henry's, Utica's best-known whorehouse. As we approach the shackling room, Victor says, "Five bucks a pop, ten for half and half, twenty-five for around the world."

That night, this dream: In a deserted area reserved for the slaughter of large or unruly animals — cows, steers, adult pigs — there my good father hangs. Upside down. Naked. Feet shackled to a ceiling hook. Victor and I in attendance. Victor says, "Look, Richard, see shackle? Say shackle, Richard." My father's eyes roll up. His mouth opens. Light pours from his head. Victor says, "Your father is a woman. Your father stinks kindness." We walk around to his backside. I say, pointing to his ass, "She always turns the other cheek." Victor says, "Oh, oh, that's rich, Richard." I say, "I want my daddy to sing for me." Victor says, "Behold! A piano! Do you wish to accompany your father? Take this piano." He gives me a big knife. "Across the throat and deep," he says. "But if you cut the head off, your daddy won't sing for you. Play the piano, Richie." Victor waves his arms like a conductor. I approach the hanged man, who says, "Play the piano deep, but not too deep, my son." Victor says, "He wants to lave you all over richly with his voice." I slash my father deep across the throat, but not too deep. A voice of shattering size flows forth, tearing the roof off, sustaining itself over the city, and as his blood pours down, a ravishing diminuendo, as his blood pours all the way down to no more bloodvoice, good to the last drop. Sun from out of the night sky and from my father's head. His genitals are a floating flower. Victor says, "He's in heaven." I say, "The cunt escaped." Victor says, "Pick the flower, forget him not." Victor is holding high a broken beer bottle, opening and neck preserved. Victor is saying, "A kid your age without condom-knowledge. Behold! This is a condom! First we put our precious peckers in here, where we drink, and only then do we do our fucking. Doobydo. The jagged edge is your protection. This jagged edge goes into the woman, in order to prevent pregnancy. Now you have condom-knowledge! Repeat after me: Peter Pecker probed a peck of prickly pussy!" I'm hanging upside down, my genitals are a broken beer bottle. Victor dips a cannoli into my father's blood. He says, "Open wide, Richard." The blood sings gloriously. Victor says, "I said, Open up, Richard, or I'll lance your secret boil." Victor is holding up a volume of the *Encyclopaedia Britannica*, the letter *K*. He says, "*K* is for killing and for Keats. Richard, Richard, a thing of beauty is a joy forever." I open wide.

The shackler is a skinny black kid who is saying "Hello, Mr. G" and pulling a thing off a wall, a long chain with a hook on one end and an iron wheel on the other, and quickly around the calf's back legs he slips and wraps it snug in a second, hooking the chain onto itself, engaging the wheel end with a thing that ascends and descends constantly. The calf goes up. The wheel rolls onto an elevated rail. The calf sails quietly through an opening in the wall, dangling down, rolling toward the killing floor, toward the first station, where the bleeder, a lugubrious white guy, awaits his work, rubber-suited, iron-wristed. Victor says, "That thing with the wheel is called the shackle. That thing that goes up and down constantly is called the hoist. You are called the future shackler, who feeds my boys out there, who have constant hunger. The shackler doesn't feed steadily, the knifemen stand around with their knives. Next thing you know, they're thinking too much about the shackling room. Richard, the shackler is a relentless person, like Nelson here, my only Negro employee, who I give this sensitive job to because he's like you. Your build, no skill, and what woman looks at him twice?" The shackling room is tiny. We can't move. The calves can't move. "The purpose is to pack them in here like sardines. As the shackler, you move only with great difficulty. But you kick freely, or preferably you deploy the heavy wheel part of the shackle like a club, on the head, or preferably the fucking spine. Like Nelson's doing now. You induce paralysis, they don't break your balls anymore." The calf is sailing toward the lugubrious bleeder. "Pack them in without mercy, send them on their way, the room empties, etcetera. In four hours, Richard, which you work per Saturday and Sunday, three hundred closures, thanks to you. You know what you're doing here? You're reaching out to the people of New York City, think of it in those terms. Not to mention the rare opportunity for deep self-expression with impunity. Naturally, all you'll ever think about in here is the knifemen, a level you'll never reach, because that takes craft plus the union. Frustration alone will not get you through a shift as a knifeman. Richard, notice those three big ones over there in the corner in the 150-pound category. They go last. Always last, or else you create a jam in the line. More aggravation for my knifemen. Those bigger bastards watch you like a hawk while you do the small ones. In my opinion, they absorb the experience. They see the future. When their time comes, if you bend down behind them without caution, a kick in the face is likely. When Nelson gets to the 150-pounders, he assumes the worst. I'll put it this way: You and Nelson can't afford increased ugliness in the facial area. In other words, a heavy smash to the spine is immediately called for. I don't care, deploy your own technique when the time comes, because you have to appease yourself, after all, and I don't object to individual creativity as long as you don't get involved in a disembowelment attempt in my shackling room." Nelson's rhythm is good to look at. "These little bastards are stupid and stubborn to the point you feel they direct hostility toward you personally. The truth of this room is that the shackler wins. They always lose. Hang them up for the first station. Lift the heavy wheel easily overhead, smash it down on the spine. The pleasure of repetition. Forget emotion. Coldness is all. Your will is done, which from what Carmen tells me will be a new situation in your life."

"In other words, here I don't take shit."

"Richard, at this time you have it all over your faggot white bucks."

We move on, to the killing floor proper, to the first station, which we can't get to directly via the shackling room, unless we wish to climb into the opening through which the calves sail quietly toward the lugubrious bleeder, which we don't. We instead exit outside and come around through the main entrance, then through the coffee and pastry room supplied daily by Carmen, then onto the killing floor proper at last, into a space adjacent to the first station where the bleeder is reaching for the snout of the calf that comes sailing quietly toward him, and where the foreman, Dick Lentricchia, stands surveying the scene: "Dick, Richard Assisi, etcetera," the bleeder grasping the snout in his left hand, pulling up the head gently so that the back of the neck presents itself properly to the trajectory of the right hand descending already as the left is doing its job, the horizontal surface presenting itself properly to the bleeder precisely as the right hand makes deep vertical contact through soft butter, three quick little saws and the head is severed, the left hand flipping, gracefully tossing it into a barrel, and a waterfall of blood, so much of it in such a little animal pours down, and the left pushing the headless calf down to the second station, then reaching for another sailing snout. A two-and-a-half-second affair, if that.

Beneath the bleeder's feet, a rectangular reservoir, maybe twelve by fifteen, curb-enclosed, an eighteen-inch barrier against the blood, with a sewer in the center, invisible at the moment. Nelson feeds steadily. The reservoir fills to the brim. Dick the foreman in the high waders of a trout fisherman steps in with a rake which he works at the center. Reservoir recedes. Victor says, "We don't want my knifemen down the line slipping and sliding, though as far as that goes my insurance covers everything." Dick laughs and says, "Then, if that happens, we hang 'em up, finish the job, put 'em in the cooler. Those people in New York pay extra for a delicacy. They'll say it tastes just like chicken." Victor says, "It's not thicker than water, Richard. It's thicker than Jell-O. The sewer clogs. It becomes a lake in there. The fucking Red Sea." Dick says, "Is that the one where Christ walked across it?" Victor says, "I'll let you know when I get to the letter *R*. Come on, Richard, let's go down to the second station. Hey, Richard, you deaf all of a sudden?" Dick says, "He's in a trance. He's in heaven."

Three knifemen stand at the station of evisceration, another curb-enclosed area, each working a calf with a maximum longitudinal rip, a couple of quick moves, a yank, and the guts just can't wait to fall out. Ambience of shit stench. Victor says, "Strictly guts and assholes. When the shackler runs out of work he comes here and shovels the guts into those barrels. It gets deep in there. In the beginning, Nelson, who is quite sensitive, shoveled. Now he's acclimated, now he uses his hands. Quicker that way. They tend to slide off the shovel. No gloves, by the way. They just get soaked in a minute. You'll begin with the shovel, proceed to the gloves. Then you'll see the point of bare hands. You'll wash your hands a lot. After a week, you'll give them a fast rinse without soap and wipe them on your pants on the way to your coffee break. You'll eat your pastries with semi-disgusting hands, mark my words, as you inhale what's under your fingernails. You'll find a level of comfort in here."

We work ourselves on down the line to the last station, the washing and the scrubbing, the wheeling of the carcasses into the cooler. Victor says, "From Nelson to the cooler, maybe a minute and a half Okay, Dick, we're ready." I follow them into a remote area, quiet, partitioned off. Dick disappears. Dick reappears leading a huge pig on a rope. Maybe 350 pounds. Dick gives the rope to Victor. Dick switches off the lights. Victor says, "Because pigs are the smartest of them all." A snort in the dark. Machinery engaged. Lights on. The pig is hanging from the ceiling. The pig urinates upon itself. Dick disappears again. Victor says, "Get ready." Dick appears with a dripping bleeder's knife. Dick holds the knife under the snout. The pig defecates massively upon itself. Victor says, "Dick, it's been years." Dick says, "Victor, I'd be honored to watch you work again." Victor slashes the pig's throat. Sound of shattering size. Victor grins. He says, "Behold! The fat lady sings! Come on, Richard, let's go across the street. I believe you're ready now for your first piece of ass."

FROM THE MUSIC OF THE INFERNO (1999)

The boy shivers nude in the dark, preparing himself on his eighteenth birthday, this fatal day in the winter of '54, preparing for what, he doesn't know, in longjohns, two pair of socks, woolen shirt, woolen pants, sweater heavier than pants, ragged black overcoat — heavier than everything. Into one pocket, a red scarf and a half loaf of Italian bread. Into the other, a jar of peanut butter and a hefty jack-knife. Laces up an outsized pair of baseball cleats, then to the belt of his long black coat secures with a giant safety pin his game bag — a burlap sack hanging to the ankles, blood-stained and feather-matted within: traces of his offerings to Caterina Spina. Breakfast? He'll eat snow. He'll suck on glittering icicles, hanging from the depressed boughs of pine trees. Pulls on a pair of white cloth gloves as he glances to the far corner of the eight by eight room. Leaning there, the offering of Gregorio Spina: a twelve-gauge shotgun. Pulls down over the ears, down low over the forehead, a hand-knitted white watch cap, the Christmas gift of Melvina Reed. Looks into the long darkened mirror attached to the closet door and a huge frightening figure, the man he wants to be, looks obscurely back. The boy in the dark feels the onset of a distant pleasure. He'll take the shotgun. On his way out when he remembers. Clomps back in and without removing the useless gloves, brushes his teeth with the fury of one who would draw blood.

This boy is a Utica boy, who believes his name to be a fake, a boy known as Robert Tagliaferro. So slight of build is he, that when properly attired for a deep winter's hunt, the weight of clothes and shotgun together become nearly too much to bear.

Already, at eighteen, he's a legendary woodsman, a deadeye who in the off-season had become a mushroomer so good that Gregorio Spina, east Utica's acknowledged King of Mushrooms, regularly invites him to explore his royal secret places in the hills around the city. "A future murderer," Spina had remarked of him happily to his wife. "I will lie to this orphan and tell him that he is my true son, and that he should live with us. Then when we are too old, he will save us from these cretins who were born with us in Italy, and who now destroy this beautiful city. Let the cretins go back to Shitland!" And his wife had replied, "Yes, let them go back. They disgust me too. But he is not dark enough. To be your son he would need to be more dark." Then Gregorio said, "I believe that he will surprise everybody. Except me. But who cares? By then I will be fucked in the cemetery! More dark? He could not be more dark."

The couple that the boy lives with in an awful tenement, in an ethnically confused section of Utica, are named Melvina and Morris Reed. He calls these good people Aunt and Uncle, who had carried him, they said, in his infancy to Utica. When asked, for the first time, where he was carried from, the Reeds had replied, insanely, that they didn't know. The second time (there would be no third), they said, "From some place else. Why does it matter? You were carried. You're here." They said, "This is the place. This is your place. "

In the exhilarating dawn of the hopeless hunt, the Reeds sleep. The Reeds, who are black. The boy, who is ambiguous, and feels his ambiguity, but cannot plumb it, and so regards himself as an inexplicable freak. "In my aspect and in my eyes," he'll learn to say, "you behold all that's best of dark and bright." "Beware," he'll learn to say with a sly small smile, "Tagliaferro comes down like the wolf on the fold." But at eighteen he has not yet learned sufficient craft to frighten with phrases, and with stories to deliver punishment.

The place said to be the boy's is located on the edge of the Italian east side of town, in an area squeezed brutally between Bleecker and Broad, south and north, and running but six short blocks, east and west. In his "Historical Notebook of Utica, New York and New York State in General," volume one, Robert would name it, many years later, the wedge. Bleecker: Italian-American Main Street of immigrant merchant princes, led by the nine brothers Cesso, whose ancient family motto was: "We come; we squat; we conquer," and who cheat their friends and even their own aunts and uncles and cousins more easily and frequently than strangers, because true friends and family, stated Primo Cesso, Cesso the First, as historians of Utica refer to him, are too loving to suspect us, and if they do, they are too kind to tell the police. And Broad, with its condemned warehouses, its empty lots of high weeds and abandoned sofas, love seats for sentimental rapists — a street of drifting trash that the people of the wedge are not tempted to walk after dark and that causes the boy to discover the comforts of his place, because there is no other, home to mostly welfare whites named Bagg, Stiggins, Sherman and Wragg.

Only the boy among them much ventures to the south side of Bleecker, to Mary Street and Spina's domain. Because he has more than the proper sort of surname. He has the looks of a beautiful bronze-toned Neapolitan waif — the sweetness, the curls — and the desire, for as long as he can recall, to live on Mary Street, a move he's suggested many times to Melvina and Morris. To which the Uncle always responds, "Somebody someday is going to mess up your pretty face." And to which the Aunt always responds, "In our colored skin? Honey, not even you could fool those people up there. So what that you're lighter than that Spina's Sicilian son-in-law, who he calls The African? Does that so-called African like to be called The African? They know who you are. Those people specialize in knowing who everybody is who is not their own selves. Because they intend to keep it intact. Follow me? Know the word hymen, hon? That's what they believe in." Robert only says, "You'll see. I'm going to buy Gregorio's house." Melvina says, "When, hon?" Robert says, "Ask Uncle Morris." Uncle Morris says, "When he's pretty no more."

Still dark: bone dry and windless. The temperature in the Mohawk Valley refuses to rise above zero. Shotgun shouldered, the boy descends into streets barely trod for a week and begins the long southerly ascent from Utica's topographical low point, the paved-over swamp land of the city's original site, up Bacon, crossing Bleecker, always rising as he crosses Mary, Blandina, Lansing, arrogant Rutger, always higher through levels of increasingly valuable real estate. At last Eagle, then left and due east to the vast rolling public park on Utica's border, crossing stooped over the park's snow fields frozen deep — a speck of black in a sea of white, this is how he prefers to see himself, in the pleasure of his solitude: as if from above, free, staring down upon himself, watching from his still point a black speck moving across desolate sheets of ice. He hugs this image of himself tight, sinks into it, thinking of nothing as he trudges almost contentedly, always east, to the area where Starch Factory Creek skirts the park's far edge, where he'll follow the creek's course up steep Albany Hill, this is the plan, on this of all days, this the object of the hunt: to reach the creek's source, hewing to the snaking course, now inside, now outside city limits, and Robert working hard against his desire to imagine the origin even as he seeks the origin, as if forethought itself were a contaminant.

His cleats dig in good. He climbs through a brushy and wooded terrain, skirting treacherous small chasms in the paradise he had discovered the summer before, in late August. He liked that word very much: discover. He felt, when he discovered it, the same way he'd felt that one time when he stood on the small second floor back porch of Gregorio's house, and there were no sounds of voices, or automobiles, or dogs, or even birds, and he could almost touch the massive fruit of the cherry tree arching over toward him, and he could stare down endlessly into the rich little garden, dense with tomatoes, lettuce, and basil, and the rusted tin roof of the shed directly below, between the garden and the house. What was he discovering then? When he told Morris, Morris said, "The shed? Is that what they call the slave quarters?" He didn't tell Morris, because he didn't have the words then, that on Gregorio's back porch, in the silence, he was the only one alive in the whole world, and how good that felt, and how he never felt better, because he was himself the cherry tree, the garden, and the shed, the only one alive.

This lonely place on Albany Hill is too rugged for real estate developers; too ambiguously related to Utica proper for hunters to take a chance; unthinkable for self-respecting trout fishermen; impossible even for Italian picnickers, for whom all pastoral places are potential sites; and ignored, thank God, by those ball-breaking teenagers who come to the park for the purpose of irritating old lady dandelion pickers with drag racing and ceaseless baseball playing, and with shouted obscenities embarrassing all the young lovers parked under the stately elms.

What were the words he had learned in his American history class at Thomas R. Proctor High? Virgin land. He's traversing "virgin land." The history teacher said that "virgin land" was what our country was before "our forefathers came." He wanted to ask his teacher (who was an Italian-American), "Whose forefathers? And who were the foremothers they came into?" Mischievously, in his bad Italian, he told Gregorio about our forefathers who came into virgin land. In dialect, Gregorio shot back, "Must I tell you what a virgin is for?" When he asked Gregorio if they, our first fuckers, had done the job to him, Gregorio, in culo, Gregorio nodded, and said: "Why do you think we came to this country, if not for that? In the old country we had no chance. Here, in America, we must spread ourselves wide open, but here we too have the opportunity to become fuckers. America is very beautiful."

These cleats, his greatest idea. Morris's cleats. The shoes of not his father. They called the park Proctor. In Utica, they called many things Proctor. Who were Bleecker, Mary, Blandina, Lansing, and Rutger? Where he was now had no name. Working on up the slope, he saw nothing, and was glad. In this terrific cold, only a single, relentless crow. Who gets to say what the names of places will be? That would be something: to become a namer of places. The previous August he'd been thrilled by the density of wild life that he'd encountered in such a small area, never hunted, not even by stray dogs. If he saw a stray dog today in his secret place, for sure he'd shoot it. Now, when he wanted none of the things of August, a jumping brown burst beneath his feet! a streak of brown streaking! and he blasts barrel one and no change of speed and he blasts barrel two: the rabbit tumbles. He approaches to verify what he suspects. That he's shot badly and must now do what he did when he began to hunt at twelve, and shot badly all the time. Hoists the quivering thing by the back legs. Delivers a swift sharp chop to the back of the neck, to grant the mercy of a broken neck, not to sever the head, which is not possible to do, but it happens: a slash of red across the white-gloved left palm, the head sliding slowly down ice, down into the creek. For her cacciatore sauce, Caterina will not require the head. To insure freshness, he slits it open all the way to and through the bung hole, removes gloves, rips out guts and tosses them into the creek, so that the guts might join the lonely head, he'll tell Gregorio, who will feel grief for the rabbit even as he forks it down with gusto. Bunny into burlap sack, safe, where it'll freeze rock-hard within an hour. Wipes his hands on the long black coat and resumes his trek, feeling a little depressed, maybe everything was ruined now, not because of what he'd done but because he'd been interrupted. Worse, because he'd let himself become involved in the interruption. Has difficulty feeling his fingers. Wraps the scarf about his face. Hides Gregorio's shotgun under a large bush. Jams his hands into his coat pockets and starts the ascent again, leaning relaxed and deep into the hill, rabbit carcass flopping against the ice. The scarf-mask is not enough. Sharp increase in the angle of ascent; radical narrowing and straightening of the creek's channel. He's leaning deeper, staring into snow. Clearing, looks up and sees it in the clearing. A tiny waterfall fed by a spring that has groped its way out of the underground, twenty yards above, at the steepest point, just before Albany Hill begins to round itself gently through the breast of the summit. Even in cleats, ice and incline would defeat him at the finish. It's hands and knees now, and when he gets there, finds beside the falls, perfectly encased in a coat of clear ice formed from the water-splash, a doll in a blue dress, shoeless, on her back. The feet are blue. The ankles too. The hands are blue. The cheeks and nose are cracked and red. Eyes open. Long lashes ice-glazed. This. Almost bald. This. Robert Tagliaferro removes the scarf, the water-splash coating his left sleeve and cheek, freezing upon him almost instantly. Removes gloves. With all his might, two-fisted he's punching the air, punching the hill bloody. Picks it up, hugging it to his chest, wrapping it in the scarf, easing it, the blue baby, so stiff, down into the game bag alongside the rabbit carcass. This is her body. Who belongs to her? Pieces of downy hair and dress sticking to the ice. He wants to rescue the hair. What else could he do, in this place, on this morning? What was he supposed to do? Leave her there? Leave the hair? With exposed fingers, picks at hair in the ice, picks at dress fragments in the ice, sitting beside the falls, smearing the ice red. Game bag on his lap, dress fragments safely secured within, pushes off sliding and down he goes, screaming, quickly gaining speed out of control over bumps and clumps of brush, screaming and crashing at last to a rest still screaming against the large bush of the shotgun. Looks inside the game bag. The ice-coating has shattered; her face is turned into the rabbit's cavity. He rearranges. Covers her as best he can with the red scarf. Transfers peanut butter and bread to sack. Then for a long time stares down into the sack, his entire head almost out of sight. Melvina's white watch cap peeping out.

11:30 A.M. Reaches again the corner of Bacon and Mary. Two doors away, the Spina house, 1303 Mary Street. Gregorio, sitting at the kitchen table, has spied him walking through the alley. Robert knocks. Caterina, alerted by her husband to the visitor's identity, steps into character: "Who's there?" Gregorio, with excessive volume, says, "Our black son!" Robert responds in heavily accented English: "Santee Clothes." Then the door, dead-bolted day and night in this crime-free neighborhood, swings open wide and he enters as she grins and tells him that she's been a good Christian and deserves a present on this morning of God's wrath. He hesitates. He reaches in. Pulls out the carcass of the rabbit. She says, in mock sadness, "Only one?" Shall he do it? He reaches in. Gives her the frozen bread. Gregorio says, "In all things, my wife is impossible to satisfy." The wife replies, "I should make my husband eat this bread like a stone. I'm going to divorce him," as she pours Robert a cup of espresso and refills her husband's cup, who says: "Your coffee is no good," then takes it down in one swallow and says "Ah!" Robert says, "Yes, divorce him tomorrow in honor of your fiftieth wedding anniversary." *La commedia è finita.*

She lays before Robert an array of his favorite things: a hunk of salami, a loaf of freshly baked bread, a dish of roasted sweet peppers sunk in olive oil, a jug of Gregorio's homemade wine, and two cannoli. He says, "Please forgive me. I cannot." Dips a finger into the olive oil. Sucks it. Says again, "I cannot." She says, with real pain, "You don't like what I put on the table?" Gregorio says, "To the Devil with him, he is fasting for communion." She replies, "But he's not a Catholic," as she watches Gregorio dig into the peppers. "Pig!" she says, "you ate twenty minutes ago!" Gregorio: "I am fulfilling my pig nature. He has no appetite. How can this boy, who eats like he doesn't like to eat, be my son?" "Thank you," Robert says, in English, "now we can begin our friendship." Caterina, who has no English, asks, "What did he say?" Her husband responds, in

Italian: "He says that for our health it is much better never to have been a member of a family." Caterina says, "Look at his knuckles. They bleed."

Spends the afternoon curled about his burlap sack, on a pew at St. Anthony's, one block from home.

Late that night, carrying Morris's claw hammer, returns to 1303 Mary Street. And then this boy, who had long cradled himself in the fangs of an incurable idea — that he, himself, was a thrown-away child — hacks up with difficulty the frozen turf of the shed floor and buries the thrown-away child, his scarf, and the jar of peanut butter.

When he returns home, very late, Melvina and Morris greet him at the door in their pajamas. They couldn't imagine where he was at such an hour. "Robert, we were so afraid something happened." [Pause.] "I made you a birthday pie." Robert, looking full at the terrorized Reeds, says, "I'm sick of being treated like a baby. I'm eighteen." Melvina says, "I'll make you a chicken sandwich, hon, and there's still some chocolate pie." Robert, who hasn't eaten all day, says, "I'm not hungry." The three of them, standing in the doorway, stare at the floor. Then Morris says, "Let's leave him alone. Let's go to bed."

There had been no news reports of missing children, distraught mothers and fathers, kidnappings, ransom notes. Nobody knew, except for Robert Tagliaferro, and the parent who did it.

FROM THE ACCIDENTAL PALLBEARER (2013)

There they are — two elegantly dressed big men in a half-empty movie theater with a sticky floor — in Troy, New York, nine miles north of Albany — Albany, the asshole of New York state, a ninety mile drive south-southeast from Utica, down the Thruway whose right hand lanes in either direction approach Third World condition. Nine miles up New York state's hole, Eliot Conte and Antonio Robinson await in Troy the start of the Metropolitan Opera's high definition live telecast of the Saturday afternoon presentation. They sit there eating sandwiches made by Robinson — salami, onions, provolone, spicy mustard. They take turns swigging from a wineskin heavy with expensive Chianti, bought by Conte — a tip of the hat, he called it, to Papa Hemingway and the macho tradition of American literature. Eliot knows his American literature. They both know their opera, like a couple of old homosexuals, life long companions — these two heteros who called each other opera queens and sometimes, deliberately, just to bust balls, in the company of tough and disgusted men who feared to mock them, they called each other handsome.

Conte stares right, away from Robinson, seeing nothing as he falls fast inside himself — as his nails, with a will of their own, dig deep into his cuticles. He speaks without affect:

"I'll get you through the kids, Nancy says. Mark my words, Eliot, before this is over, I will kill our kids."

Robinson with a mouthful, "You go to Ricky's? You get the cookies from Ricky?"

"Direct quote: I will kill our kids."

"The imminent ex-to-be lamenting the imminent loss of your erotic power — nothing more."

"At the time, Robby, I was banging Nancy on a semi-yearly schedule."

"I have to say my wife would be unhappy at that pace."

"Millicent obviously requires more."

"Less."

"So I say, Nancy, how old are you? She goes, Okay, Eliot, I get it, you cocksucker. She's younger than me? Huh? She's better looking than me? This is why you're leaving me and the kids? You asshole. I say, She's twelve years older than you. She's forty-one, Nancy, and not as attractive as you, either."

"Wait a minute, Eliot. You tell her you're leaving her for what? A better person? Not a better piece of ass? You tell her you're leaving her for some older plain Jane of superior character?"

"Who said plain Jane?"

"Basically you had the balls to tell her, in so many words, you were choosing a more vibrant personality, a truly complex mind, a finer sensibility — a woman with an impeccable taste for the performing arts, who would never call you a cocksucker. All the while, Nancy assumes, as anyone with the slightest knowledge of the male gender would assume, that you, Eliot Conte, were flushing her down the toilet for a new and juicy piece who makes your cock explode. And you expected her to what? Applaud your admirable values?"

Eliot Conte, private investigator, B.A., M.A. UCLA. Antonio Robinson, Eliot's childhood friend, his only friend, who'd been a storied athlete in their high school days at Proctor and then again as a thrilling half-back at Syracuse University — now Chief of Police of their hometown, Utica, New York. Robin-

son, the city's cuddly black teddy bear — cuddled even by the older generation of Italian-American racists, who control the city's political structure.

It was, in fact, Eliot's father, eighty-eight year old Silvio Conte, a legend across
the state and a political king-maker, Silvio "Big Daddy" Conte, owner of the
flourishing Utica Prosthetics, who had pulled the strings two years ago to get
Robinson appointed Chief. Not out of the goodness of his heart. Much less
based on a judgment of professional merit. And not out of fear, either, because Silvio Conte fears no one — this visionary political artist who could
spot potential years in advance of its actualization, at which time he would
seize and twist it to his benefit. Hence, Antonio Robinson. Hence, "my special
son," Big Daddy had called him from the time his biological son and Antonio
were children and Antonio took more meals at the Conte home than his own.
Eliot had never felt like a special son. Eliot understood, as everyone in Utica
understood, in the absence of evidence — absence being the proof of truth
— that strings had been pulled. How else could Antonio have vaulted year
after year over higher ranked men all the way to the office of Chief? Eliot didn't
want the details and Antonio never offered any, and Eliot was grateful. After
all, how clean was Eliot Conte? Hadn't his father — it must have been his father who'd pulled strings on his own behalf when he'd returned from the West
Coast? When he'd failed the state examination for a PI license, but nevertheless a month after receiving the letter telling him he'd failed and could try
again in six months, he'd received a second letter from the Governor's Chief
of Staff, no less, saying with regret that a mistake had been made and please
find enclosed a fully executed license and permit to carry a concealed weapon.

Robinson, picking his teeth with the edge of his ticket, "It's been thirty
years you dumped Nancy? What's the point of raking up the past?"

"The point? I was called last night from Laguna Beach, California."

"And?"

"At 3 A.M., Robby."

"Yeah?"

"Three in the morning, Robby."

"Spit it out, Professor."

"They're holding her for questioning."

"For what?"

"The murders of my two daughters."

"You have dark comic talent."

Eliot Conte stares at his friend.

Antonio Robinson drops the wineskin.

"Slaughtered in their sleep."

Robinson cannot speak.

"Do you know what I feel, Robby?"

"Talk to me, El."

"I feel now what I've felt for thirty years about the kids. Nothing," says Conte, at his cuticles again, needing to feel nothing.

"Nothing?"

"As I walk out the door, she says, When you least expect it, asshole."

Robinson suggests they leave and find a full-service bar "because this is no time for — "

Conte cuts him off, putting his hand on Antonio's arm, "Let's stay and enjoy the performance."

"You're in shock, El. Let's go."

"No. I look forward to the last scene when Don Josè plunges his knife into her breast, down to the heart — just after they sing with such ferocious passion that it's impossible, handsome, for me to walk to the car without your assistance." (The elderly two gentlemen sitting two rows behind them, who are hard of hearing, stiffen on "handsome," though not in the right place.) "I anticipate the last scene and already my legs turn to jello."

Robinson stands, brushes crumbs off his pants, spots a nice sized fragment of provolone snagged by his breast pocket, pops it into his mouth — sucks, chews and swallows, sits again, fumbling in the brown paper bag and extremely irritated, "You go to Ricky's. You have coffee with Ricky. You two cunts bullshit for an hour. And then you forget to buy the fuckin' cookies. Listen: whether you feel anything or not, or you're repressing or not, you need to put this monster out of her misery. In cold blood."

"I don't do that."

"Not yet."

"You know I don't do that."

"Your UCLA exit, Eliot."

"What about it?"

"Demonstrates potential."

"That wasn't me."

"What they all say. Temporary insanity etcetera."

"That wasn't really me, Robby."

"Who was it, Eliot? . . . Do her the way she did your kids. As she sleeps.

Raise your game to the next level."

"If she did it."

"She did it."

"She's in custody."

"She'll walk. Trust me."

"How can you be so sure, Robby?"

"This is what we know. The worst walk."

"Like me. When I walked out on the kids. When they were babies."

"I didn't hear that. I never heard it. Man, your fuckin' cuticles are bleedin' on your pants. Listen: she walks, then you walk back in, propose marriage, and do the right thing on the first night of your second honeymoon. For twenty years, since you returned from the West Coast, you've been doing good and Utica is the better for it. Speaking of which, this Michael C thing we need to discuss at intermission is much worse than I let on. It's bad, Eliot."

As the gold curtain rises at the Met, Robinson leans over and whispers, "Time to fall in love again."

"Take a look at her, Robby — this Amazonian beauty! This is our Carmen!"

In the hush, one last pull each on the wineskin, then Robinson leans in again and whispers, "You feel something. This is your problem. It's always been your problem."

4 ◆ A Life in Art

From Lucchesi and The Whale (2001)

"Islas Malvinas"

"As we grow older," Lucchesi says at sixty, alone, at his desk, "we grow more extremely ourselves. Contact depresses us; conversation debilitates": Words spoken with forced eloquence, like a bad classical actor in an old movie. And yet, except for hiding himself behind collective pronouns, Lucchesi spoke sincerely: Forced eloquence had long since become second nature to him, there in his cramped writing room, where the writing no longer comes, and where he now makes desperate calls at all hours, to contact those he'd barely known in his early school days, and hasn't seen since. Only names now, at the farthest edge of memory; names dragging reluctant images of fresh faces, in black and white, of ten, and twelve, and fourteen year olds.

He wants to call the faces. First, all with the same surname in the town in upstate New York he'd left in his early twenties. Then directory assistance in many distant American cities, even London he calls. In futility, weeping to be told: "Oh, she died two weeks ago. Are you a close friend?" "No such listing, sorry." "I have a listing, sir, for the Federal correctional facility at Leavenworth." "Why should I talk to you? Of all people, you?" "She's dead. Where you been?" "He died." "Years ago, she moved way out West with her third husband. I can't remember the state. I think it might have been Idaho, or South Carolina." "He says to tell you that he's indisposed at the present time on the toilet, and he'll get in touch with you some time next month." "Buzz off, this is Christmas Eve." "She died." "He died." "I died." "You died. You're dead. Sorry."

And it is Christmas Eve. And he thinks of himself as Ebenezer Scrooge, not because Money is All, but because Art is All. He, Thomas Lucchesi, the Scrooge of Art, who hoards himself to writing. He gives so little to others, he gives nothing, who would now reclaim his past with words.

Speaks again: "Lucchesi weeps for Lucchesi. True. Too easily true. But true." [Takes a note.] For something more did he weep? For contact purified by nostalgia, for contact without cost, he wept. And for the change of children, the mortality of childhood, he did weep. Pathetic. Such pathetic banalities. [Takes a note.] But it was precisely that, he thought, that had lent him his tenuous hold on the chain of humanity: His tendency to weep over the banalities that bind: all that treacherous crud that he labored to expunge from his literary voice. [Expunge: Break the chain.] He wept that children should grow to become grieving adults. Wept because an abused child was happier than any adult who had not been abused, because he believes that even an abused child, which he'd not been, lives in a magical kingdom, as he does not, as do not all the children of his memory, who had surely grown to become grieving adults. [Grown: groan.] Believes death to be the other magical kingdom and adulthood a long transition of exile. In the kingdom of death, the fresh faces will meet again. Until then? If only he could write again.

Recalls her: Malvina. The one forcing her way from the far edge of memory to the center. Or was it Malvina? His dictionary of personal names gives both spellings. Much prefers the latter, doesn't know why. It'll be Malvina. Two spellings, one face: black, stern, starkly attractive, with a long bony body, fierce and flexible on the playgrounds of the eighth grade. At twelve, she, Malvina the dominant, and young Lucchesi had competed for valedictorian of their grammar school and finished in a dead heat. Of course, they'd never spoken. She'd spoken to no one, not even her teachers. Who dared speak with Malvina? Once he followed her home. Wanted to knock on the door, but didn't. Wanted to be in her stern black place, because he thought it might make him stern and romantic. Elevate him to her plane of aristocracy. Her surname had not survived. [Good: can't call.]

Now he has his house of books. He's library-sufficient [Note] and, therefore, all-sufficient [Note]. He'll build her back, out of his books. Make literary contact with an obscure Princess, for purposes of high discourse on the grave matter of her stern, stern world.

Against that day when maybe the ice would break up and thaw, he'll file his notes in a manila folder. Thinks of Malvina gestating in the folder; thinks of the Falklands War. The Falkland Islands, down at the end of the Argentine coast, 300 miles out where the Atlantic verges on the south polar region, and he's remembering a British TV correspondent stationed in Buenos Aires referring to the islands as the Malvinas. Plural. Islas Malvinas. Not since the eighth grade had Lucchesi heard that sound. What is a Malvina? His dictionary of personal names gives him Melvina, from Irish, "an armored chief" [Yes], derived perhaps from Gaelic moal-mhin, "smooth brow" [Yes]. But Malvina from Scottish was the creation of a poet, who had claimed to discover an ancient Gaelic epic: James Macpherson, oh yes! he knew of Macpherson! eighteenth-century literary fraud, so gripped by the idea of an art rooted in folk culture, in local earth, that he invented it. The scandal of Macpherson's hoax only helped Malvina do what she had long yearned to do: escape from the poem and her creator: leap from the text, leap down into the world, where many in the late eighteenth and early nineteenth centuries named their daughters Malvina. Then she slipped underground. For almost two hundred years nobody named their girl-child Malvina, until she returned, taciturn and mythic, in the imagination of a recessed and frail white boy, in the small town of Utica, New York. Malvina, foundling gift of the literary gods, in temporary residence with a poor black family living at the edge of an Italian-American neighborhood. The old Italians called her: graziadei. Local earth; local object of desire; vision. [Who needs a telephone?]

The furnace fails in Lucchesi's house; cold air blows through the vents in his writing room. Getting on to midnight. Feels a little better; new writing may be at hand.

Assumes that Islas Malvinas is Spanish. Assumes that these islands were called Malvinas originally, before they became known as the Falklands. But the encyclopedias correct him: it seems that the British, like God, were originally everywhere, and the slow collapse of Empire was like the generous, but wary, withdrawal of God, which permitted being other than His own to exist. The British, the first namers, baptized the islands after one of their Naval commanders. Then the islands were settled by the French who, in the arrogance by which the world would come to know them, refused to make a variant of "Falklands" in their language. The French decided, instead, to express themselves. They decided: Lucchesi loves the idea. [Takes a note.] Because they needed to think of themselves as the first namers. And so they called them Isles Malouines. And then the belated Spanish, whose Islas Malvinas was indeed a Spanish variant on Isles Malouines. Spanish ruthlessness was tempered by lack of original genius. [Brits? French? Spanish? Kindergartners in the Imperialism of Art.] But what was signified by the French imagination? Malouines? What were they? The encyclopedists say that the original settlers were from Saint Malo, and that Malouines was "no doubt" (encyclopedists imagine too) the feminine diminutive in Old French of Malo. But malo in Lucchesi's dictionary of Old French doesn't exist, though the list of "mal" words is immense.

Lucchesi decides to express himself. Writes: "These islands are small. 'Saint' in old French is figurative for 'inner sanctum.' The Falklands, the inner sanctum of small evils? So I compose; so I would compose myself on my small island, this writing room."

Like Lucchesi, the Malvinas are not arable. They are treeless, and monotonously bleak, except for the millions of penguins which journey up from the neighboring ice world of Antarctica to mate. [Cold Copulars!] Mean temperature: 42° Fahrenheit, with winds constant from all directions at twenty miles per hour, periodically sustained at gale force. Lucchesi thinks about the wind chill factor. Lucchesi feels no chill. Rain and snow 200 days per year. Shore line cut deep by fjords. Makes a note: "Like Norway in the South Atlantic." Makes another note: "Cancel the sentiment. Cancel all sentiment." Cloud-cover virtually perpetual; fog breaking on occasion to reveal, in patched sunlight, herds of sheep passing over brutally graveled roads, grazing unfenced, but marked by their owners with coded dyes: a slash of red, or indigo, over the shoulders, flaring out like blood through the steaming mist. Sheep to humans: 800 to 1, a ratio that pleases Lucchesi greatly. He makes a note of it. Principal import: alcoholic beverages, of course. Lucchesi adds to the fact: "and countless reams of typing paper, so that the humans can fight back against the fucking sheep." Coastal topography: drowned river valleys.

Long ago, East Falkland served as a whaling station, the last before the tall ships, mainly American, in penetrating enterprise rounded Cape Horn and made for the Marquesas, Tahiti, and the rich Japanese cruising grounds: And Lucchesi delights to imagine him there, Melville, of course, ruddiest of writers, strolling in the Malvinas! Strolling beaches of white quartz sand and suddenly seized by impulse, stripping, and plunging out of sight into the frigid surf, to dare the giant kelp coils: Look! Melville's swimming too far out, he's diving too deep! Herman! Don't come up! There! There it is again, the bold bearded head bobbing among the white caps, to stare down blank dramatic sea cliffs, and the vast rolling moors of this awful waste.

In a geographical survey of the saints, he finds it: Saint Malo. Named for a Welsh monk who had fled to Brittany in the sixth century to escape persecution: Maclou, which became in modern French, Malo. Nothing to do with evil, everything to do with silence and rejection of the world which insisted on taking an interest in the monk. Lucchesi smiles in his cold room. Writes: "Am I not, in a way, more like Christ than I am like Scrooge? Have I not renounced all for Art? The Scrooge-Christ of Art, who has hoarded his self to Writing the Father. And not gained the world. Because who buys his books? And lost his soul. Wherein lie all my profits?"

Lucchesi feels very good. No chance he'll weep now. Raises window high to let in a blast of icy air. Inhales deep. The heat had long gone down, and now the electrical power goes too, and he's in the dark, in the House of Books, without a single candle, just as he was about to begin new work at last, the first sentences stirring in his mind. He'll have to write in the mind. In the dark in his mind: "Writing is taking place." [Revises:] "Writing takes the place. In the Malvinas, something fast in the white grass. Arms up. Racing with her arms up, fists clenched, hair whipped back in the wind, a black streak through white grass. Secret, self-contained, solitary: We take the place, Malvina and I."

He'll memorize it. Revise in the mind through the night. Memorize the revision, waiting for dawn. Happy in his unredeemed state. No doubt about it: quite happy.

Time to tear the telephone from the wall.

"THE FAN CLUB"

Thomas Lucchesi finds himself on the busiest street corner in his hometown, where he sees a woman in the far distance come running, directly at him she comes, with something in her hand. She closes in, pointing something, haggard and middle-aged. He freezes. She collapses at his feet, dead. In her hand, a book of indeterminate authorship. A policeman rushes to the scene, but before he can speak, Lucchesi says, "It's nothing. It's just my wife." The policeman says, "She's nothing?" Lucchesi says, "Correction. It's nothing." The policeman says, "Sorry to disturb you, sir." Then pointing to the heap, the policeman says, "What would you like me to do with this?" Lucchesi responds, "Leave it. I might put it in a vase."

A crowd gathers. Among them, two faces familiar to Lucchesi from an old family album: his parents on their honeymoon. Lucchesi says, "I know you." The man extends his hand: "Hello, I'm Thomas Lucchesi." Lucchesi says, "Senior. You're Thomas Lucchesi senior. I'm young Tom, I'm junior." Senior says, "How disgusting." The woman addresses junior: "Are you cracking up, or what?" Senior says, "Your angles are all off, mister." Lucchesi says, "Which angles?" Senior answers, "Don't play dumb, buddy. I'm tired of your antics." Junior says, "Will you please hug me now, please?" The man and the woman hug each other and kiss deeply. Junior says, "No! Me! Me! HUG me! I'm your son." They stare at him. "Goddamn it," he says, "I'm going to be your son." Senior says, "You want us to make you?" Junior says, "You will make me." Senior says, "You're a cocky bastard." The woman adds, "You must be pushing sixty, for God's sake! Are you trying to induce a double suicide?" The man says to his beautiful new wife, "What do you say, Ann? Shall we make him?" Ann points to the dead woman and says, "You get involved with this character, this is where it leads." The dead woman says, "Don't kid yourself. I'm better off." The man says, "What do you say, Ann?" Ann says, "I'm game." Lucchesi senior picks up the book of indeterminate authorship and says, "Before we make you, I need to ask you a question. Did you write this thing?" Junior says, "Don't you like me?" Ann says, "Quick! Let's commit double suicide." The man and the woman eat of the book. They collapse. The policeman rushes back. He says, "Who are these dead people, sir?" Lucchesi replies, "They all throw themselves at my feet. My greatest fans."

"A NIGHT AT THE OPERA"

When the obscure American novelist, Thomas Lucchesi, checks in at the Alitalia counter, he's told that he's been upgraded to First class, at no extra charge. After he boards, he's presented with a rare edition of the score of La Bohème. Flabbergasted, he says to the flight attendant, "Tomorrow evening I'll be at La Scala, to hear this very opera, with Pavarotti himself. The sound of his name alone thrills me." The fetching flight attendant replies, "Not as much as the sound of Lucchesi thrills me, sir." He says, "You've read me?!" She says, "Why not?"

At La Scala, they don't give him the seat that he'd paid through the nose for, but one deep in the orchestra, adjacent to an exit. When he complains, the elegant usher says, "In due course, sir." Minutes before the curtain, depressed, he hears the announcement: "Mr. Lucchesi. Mr. Thomas Lucchesi. Please report back stage immediately." The usher, who has all along been standing at the exit, with an eye trained on the writer, escorts him briskly back stage, saying, as they go: "Now, sir, while there is still time!" Lucchesi, surly, says, "Now what?" They are met by the artistic director, who tells Lucchesi that Pavarotti is indisposed and that he, Mr. Thomas Lucchesi, will have to step in. "Because you have no choice. All of Milan trembles." The usher says, "See? You should have vocalized when I told you to!" The cast gathers round him. Lucchesi whimpers, "But I'm not a tenor." To which the baritone snorts, "You're not even a singer, you arrogant bastard." Lucchesi responds (sotto voce), "I am only a writer." The artistic director says, "Good! The role of Rodolfo is that of a writer. In Bohème, Pavarotti sings a writer." Lucchesi says, "I could write a singer, perhaps, but I cannot *sing* a singer. Besides, I'm a baritone. More or less." The disgusted baritone says, "A barreltone? You? Do you have a massive dark understructure?" The soprano adds, hornily, "Do you? Do you have a massive dark understructure? All true barreltones do." The semi-tumescent artistic director says, "Sir! You know this music better than you know your so-called self. Make every effort to breathe naturally and your voice will be buoyed-up as upon a great cushion, your voice will spring as upon a trampoline! Breathe from the very balls of you, sir! We want the bright, the focused, the ringing top. Mr. Lucchesi! Remember nature!"

Then from everywhere he hears the pouring of that warm, familiar ocean of sound, in full flood, and he's laved all over by an intimacy plunged deep, insistent: Lucchesi is beside his so-called self. The Tenor appears: happy, as always. Lucchesi says, "That was not indisposed, Luciano." The baritone says, "You're on a first-name basis with him?" The Tenor, grinning, says, "Thomas, I am bored. Lately, I fear that I have begun to sing a singer singing beautifully." The Tenor hears the soprano whisper, "They're on a first-name basis with each other," and The Tenor replies, "It is always the way when we love an artist. We say Dante. We say Michelangelo. We say Elvis." Startled, Lucchesi says, "You've read me too?!" The artistic director, in full tumescence now, trots out front to announce the replacement for The Tenor. The Tenor says, "Why not? The fetching flight attendant and I discuss your books during those long dead hours over the North Atlantic, when the plane seems fixed forever in the sky, and land is hopeless. Then we have you. Only you." From the house a roar, signifying either hope or horror. The Tenor continues, "All of Milan trembles.

Over the North Atlantic we do not have enough of you. We love you. But we desire to love you more, if only you would permit it. No, you cannot sing a singer. I agree. Nor can I. I sing. Over the North Atlantic we discuss your subtle disease. My dear Thomas, you write a writing, and this is why the total animality of your style is withheld just enough to rob us of your best. I sing. Write! Let your brain become as dumb and cold as a trout in a remote alpine stream, in mid-winter. Because this is what your brain most desires. Then write! And your passion will fatten and flame on the page and we will scream over the North Atlantic: LuuuuuCCHEsi! LuuuuuuuCCHEsi!"

The writer says, "Luciano! I'm not a tenor!" The soprano says to the baritone, "What's that puddle at his feet?" The baritone says, "The arrogant bastard peed his pants." Lucchesi says, "Luciano! Look! I peed!" The Tenor replies, "Thomas, you pee; before every performance, I puke. Then I jump in and they go crazy." Lucchesi says, "Everyday, before I write, I puke." The Tenor puts his arm around Lucchesi and says, "We are the same. We are exactly the same. Thomas! Jump mindlessly into your own warm ocean and all of Milan will scream."

The usher requests, and is granted, Lucchesi's autograph. The Tenor, grinning again, says, "I need to be replaced." The stage manager leads Thomas Lucchesi, a new tenor, to his mark on the first act set.

Curtain going up.

"ON HOLIDAY"

I'm in between medical appointments, and Barnes & Noble happens to be located in between. I'm eating a half-sandwich of grilled vegetables, drinking a small bottle of alpine spring water, when he spots me: a clerk, my long-absent next-door neighbor. He says, as he sits, "Tom, may I join you?" I say, "If you must." He says, "You probably noticed that I separated from my wife." I say, "I never noticed." He says, "The bone in her throat was, I rolled over in bed and hit her." I say, "I'm sorry." He says, "It was an accident. You still writing those books?" I say, "I'm in between unpublished books. I'm relaxing." He says, "Oh." I avert my gaze. He says, "To be honest, it's a case of domestic violence. You probably heard her scream." I say, "My ears ring constantly. It's a permanent condition." He says, "I hit her twice in church." I say, "Accidentally?" He says, "I'm a lucky man. My wife loves me." I look down at my plate and say, "So you're working here now." He says, "I'm reading all the books. How come they don't have any of yours?" I look up. He says, "You look tired. Are you sick?" I say, "I was sick. I'm okay now. I'm relaxing." He says, "Did you ever hit your wife?" I say, "As you no doubt recall, I'm not married. Nor have I ever been married." He says, "Don't get snotty with me. I'm bigger than you. I'm bigger." I say, "I'm sorry." He says, "Does your wife love you?" I say, "Yes." He says, "That didn't stop me, did it?" I say, "Why should love have to bear that burden?" My neighbor rises and says, "Before I go, tell me the name of that book you supposedly finished." He extends his hand. From my sitting position, I shake his hand, and say, "The Joy of Writing." He says, "Whatever you had, my friend, you're not over it."

"Moral Turpitude 101"

In the beginning, the Dean said, "No problem, he's artistic, etcetera. Forget it, he's tenured," when a student reported to him that Lucchesi had begun the Fall semester by telling his seminar in classic American literature, "I'm only here because my fiction is commercially untouchable. Never forget that. Number two: Let's do our best not to assassinate Hawthorne and Melville. Apropos of which, I intend to subject you to repeated and strenuous exercise in deep aesthetic immersion." Thereafter, each of his fifty-minute class hours started with an exceedingly slow call of the roll, a kind of chant, followed by a twenty-two minute silence, during which Lucchesi stared at a closed text and muttered occasionally, but rhythmically, "I am all the way under. Are you?"

When the Dean was called in by the President, he said, "As friends of the arts, we're not concerned. We have him surrounded. In addition, Jan, his humorous public readings bring town to gown." President Jan replied, "Community penetration?" The Dean said, "Yes. And the town, the Italian-Americans who run this crappy town, are pleased to see him gleam at his public readings. He's the Italian-American jewel in our multicultural crown. His paesanos, of course, quietly loathe him. The man is unpublishable. He needs us, Jan. We contain multitudes."

But when Lucchesi told his class on Dickinson and Whitman, apropos of nothing, that he'd once worked in a lingerie boutique, and that he'd achieved "celebrity on the mall" for his finely honed skill in the line of the "hand-fitted leotard," the Dean felt forced to call him in. Lucchesi told the Dean to "forget about it," because he'd made it all up, he was merely "trying out" a comic scene in his novel-in-progress and wanted to test the impact of the key phrase. The Dean nodded and said, "Market research." Then the Dean coughed and laughed simultaneously, raunchily, as he spit up "hand-fitted leotard." Lucchesi, still expressionless, told the Dean that artists on the faculty had the same need as traditional scholars: to integrate teaching and research, in order to make the classroom experience "whole again beyond confusion." The Dean said, "Cut the bullshit. I'm going to let this one go, you son of a bitch, because I happen to personally like you."

Finally, late in the semester, in his seminar on Moby-Dick, Lucchesi disappeared for three weeks, telling his Chairperson that he thought he was dying. When he returned, he told the class, "I was, and continue to be, terminally sick of myself. Nevertheless, while at home, I managed to bulldoze my way joyfully through a seventh draft of my experimental novel." Then he picked up the fat text of Moby-Dick, waved it high overhead, and screamed, "I have no idea what this is. Do you? Answer me! I AM AFRAID! I AM AFRAID OF THIS COCKSUCKER!!" Formal complaints were lodged by campus feminists, gays, and bi-sexuals, with the enthusiastic endorsement of a new group, which called itself: Numerous Big Straight Males. The Dean told him, "I'm sorry, Thomas, but my back is up against the wall. I'm sorry because you know how I feel. Unfortunately, you deployed a certain word pejoratively. You put yourself outside the sexual epicenter. Because it is equally good to give and to receive. Asshole." Then the Dean giggled. Then the Dean made a large obscene gesture and they both giggled. "From the Christian point of view," Lucchesi said, "it is better to give than to receive. Are you not, sir, a practicing Christian?" Laughing hard, the Dean embraces Lucchesi and says, "I am so sorry, because I just love your artistic orientation."

5 ◆ The Rookie Professor

From The Sadness of Antonioni (2011)

A voice from behind, like a warm bath, and a gentle hand on my shoulder — I turn around and there he is, Jack Del Piero himself — there we are at the Provost's annual party for new faculty, one week before the start of the Fall semester at the College of Western Connecticut, where I'm to assume a post in the Program for Theoretical Meditation on Film and Video. They know me at the College as Hank Morelli, freshly minted Ph.D. out of the University of Chicago — twenty-six years old, with a prize-winning dissertation on "The Crisis of Temporality in the Cinema of Michelangelo Antonioni." I know myself as lonely and hungry for adventure after too many years in the library. Indisputably, the program was Del Piero's, to which he'd improbably ascended to the chairmanship, seven years before, following the sudden death of the Program's gigantic founding chair — Big Fred Ozaki, a man whose critical works were still revered and condemned across several continents.

The next day, as he showed me about campus, he told me how much he appreciated my reaction to his initial greeting. As he put it, his "doing me from behind." It pleased Jack greatly to imply that he was homosexual. Near the end, I asked him why. He shrugged his shoulders and replied, "Why not?"

"Usually new faculty tell me with their first glance they know me by reputation, they're honored to meet me, they're in awe, a little in awe, and though I've been dead for thirty years they nevertheless detect the lingering bouquet of putrefaction. A little in awe? Formerly so. With a glance, they tell me they're unsuccessfully, with devastating embarrassment to themselves, trying to suppress embarrassment on my behalf. They say all these things in a first glance, then quickly flee me, 'Excuse me, sir, can you tell me where I can find the women's room? I need to vomit my guts out.' Is it obvious, Hank? I'm the College's star paranoid. You, on the other hand . . ."

He breaks off midstream — not reaching for the precise word, but distracted, or maybe liberated. I prefer to think liberated. From himself. (As if I knew.) Del Piero drifting off to the good place behind his eyes. (So I hope: a good place for Del Piero.) He comes back from wherever he's gone.

"You didn't do awe, Hank, you did actual open-faced interest — you oozed sincerity, forgive my tone. Haven't had open-faced interest since Big Fred died. Your childlike innocence is a terminal illness. Mark my words, kid, you'll get the ladies but you can't save yourself — children never can. Some broad is going to eat you alive." He takes me by the arm and says, "Me? I'm darkness visible," grinning, "which is why I've got Nadia. Would you like to meet Nadia? She calls herself Nadia."

At the instant of Jack's approach, the crowd scurries from us radially like cockroaches when you turn on the light in your kitchen at three in the morning. Okay? Now you know all you need to know about the academy-loathing attitudes that bonded Jack and me, two academic self-loathers. Del Piero, who flashed and disappeared in the avant-garde sky so long ago.

He had exactly a year and a half to his credit at Haverford College when, on the day of his twentieth birthday, he left and broke through with four films in four years. Then, at twenty-five, he begins the journey to oblivion. No more interviews. No more public appearances. Silence — even as his experiments in pornography are honored at Cannes, Venice, and Toronto for "the beauty of their images and an original cinematic language," while being denounced by Cardinals and daytime talk show hosts for the usual reasons. When Jack is twenty-eight, Ozaki's landmark philosophical meditation on his films appears, The Pornography of Everyday Life: Notes on the Structure of Postmodern Beauty, an international sensation, which ensures Jack's place in the history of film and the tenured position at the College that Ozaki secures for him when Jack is twenty-nine. When I met him, he was just shy of his sixty-second birthday.

The College of Western Connecticut is not, obviously, Harvard or Stanford — schools that wouldn't touch Ozaki with a ten foot pole, whose book, though widely read, debated, and occasionally venerated, was scorned at the old elite places as "original nonsense." Ozaki's sexual tourism (his true cachet) was so outrageous that it got him noticed regularly in People magazine and Vanity Fair, where he was once referred to as "King Stud, all 350 pounds of him." The Provost, a bottomless consumer of celebrity gossip, hires Ozaki, then Del Piero, after which he makes the decision to pour disproportionately the College's limited resources into Film and Video, to the lasting resentment of all other departments. The Program becomes the College's flagship, the place where all ambitious film studies scholars want to be. As a consequence, this nowhere school without a history (founded in 1967) awakes to find itself prominently on the academic map. When I told my mother what I was being paid, she said, "Don't tell nobody."

The roaches retreat to the walls of the Provost's reception hall and Jack and I are left alone at the center like newlyweds at the postnuptial celebration, to dance, all eyes upon us, our final dance before leaving for the honeymoon — the Provost circling, nodding and smiling, the happy father and mother of the bride and groom rolled into one. He utters a long sentence, declaimed in operatic Italian, ever circling. Neither of us understand. Not even a word. He tells us that we're his Italian-American trump cards in the great American diversity show. We were (still circling us, very drunk) his "Negro equivalents, so why should I hire any more of those people?" Jack and I thought of ourselves as ex-Italian-Americans who'd broken out of prison, though neither of us, truth be told, had ever done a minute of ethnic hard time.

I must correct two impressions that I've given you. 1) That Del Piero was a great talker. He was not. His self-lacerating monologues were infrequent, if mordantly brilliant, interruptions of long silences and longer yet times of periodic grunts and one or two word ejaculations. I exaggerate to make a point. The man taught to great acclaim, though it was hard to imagine him actually functioning in the classroom. The Program's meetings he chaired rarely exceeded fifteen minutes — no exaggeration — and his memos were virtually non-existent. As were e-mails, faxes, and phone calls. No one complained. 2) You may think that I'm a great talker. I am not. Sure, I talk well enough about my dissertation, but only because I've memorized all the words. Otherwise, I have difficulty speaking grammatically and fear that my working oral vocabulary rises to the level of a not unusually bright eighth grader. Strip Jack and me of our official identities and you'll take us for stereotypical Italian-American dummies — Yo! Tony! — graduates, at best, of two year technical institutes. My students like and admire me, but, then, what teacher worth his fraudulence can't bamboozle his students? I like to write because when I look in the mirror of my prose I see a fluent and fluid self, a man who exists only in the magic mirror of his sentences.

The Provost staggers away and Jack says that his "theoretically-inclined colleagues" were deeply impressed by my dissertation, but that he hadn't gotten beyond the title.

"What's wrong with the movies," he says?

"What?!"

"What do you have against the movies?"

"I like the movies."

"Then why didn't you say the movies of Antonioni?"

"Oh."

"Or at least the films of?"

"Uhh . . ."

"Speak to me, Morelli."

"Gee."

"Golly jeepers creepers Morelli, something wrong with the films of?"

"I don't think so."

"You're turning red. I sympathize. We're here. Here, this is how they talk: The Crisis of Temporality in the Cinema of Michelangelo Antonioni. Christ."

"Okay."

"You want to be taken seriously. Here. By them."

"Is that a sin?"

"Yes. Never write like these people."

"I'll try not to."

"What the fuck's wrong with time?"

"I get it."

"Do you really? What's wrong with time?"

"Instead of temporality?"

"Hank, I fear those big words. They make me unhappy."

"I'm sorry."

He makes the sign of the cross.

He says, "I don't do theoretical meditation and I no longer do alcohol. Hence the club soda. And I don't go to meetings where they want you to acknowledge the bastard who doesn't exist, which is why I'm a white knuckler."

I can't respond.

"Aren't you going to respond to my intimate revelations? It's your turn. I talk you talk. Gift me with your speech."

I can't respond.

"Back and forth, Hank, like tennis."

I mime an elegant, one-handed backhand slice.

"You obviously play the game. Great backhand."

"Never played."

"Atta boy! Bet that martini's too wet. You want a proper one? Say bring me a gin martini, up, four olives, no vermouth. None. Then they put in just enough to give you truly dry. I make proper martinis for guests."

I don't respond.

"I imagine you saying you can't respond. I keep a full stock of the hard stuff. Strengthens my resolve."

"Interesting."

"You can do better than that."

"Wow!"

"Good. I miss Ozaki."

"I can imagine."

"I believe you do. I knew Antonioni in the seventies. Just before he and Monica Vitti split. She destroyed him, vice-versa. Knew her in the non-Biblical sense."

"You actually knew them?"

"He wasn't a talker. (Sort of like you.) He was a maker. She was a talker. Tremendous comedian. He sits there. Reads. Takes notes. Stares a lot. Suffers persistent low level depression. Or he doesn't read and take notes. Just sits and stares. Or paces, staring and depressed. After seventeen years of this she tells him, You bore me. He goes to the window. Hands on hips. Staring. Comic faces she made were an enormous turn on. For me. She made them for me. But I never had the nerve. Had my shot, though. Had my shot. That was back in the seventies, when I. . . . He never turns from the window to look at her. She walks out of his life and he's eviscerated. Never again makes anything worth a damn. You're thinking how does Del Piero know this? Over drinks in her apartment, while candles flicker at twilight. Self-conscious heavy petting. I thought of going down on her. That was it. Didn't have the nerve."

"I can't take my eyes off that mesmerizing mouth of hers."

"No longer the case. You don't want to know."

"Can imagine."

"Let's hope not. Alzheimer's in addition. Watch her movies, Hank."

"Alzheimer's in addition to the ever-enlarging disasters of her body. Her time-ravaged face."

"Did you have to spell it out? Have you no decency, sir? Took her seventeen years to realize she was bored. Bitch."

"Maybe it snuck up on her, the boredom, from close behind, late in year sixteen. The boredom did her from behind."

"How to go, Hank!"

He says, "I seriously screened his great stuff — of the early Vitti period —

after we met. Killed my desire to make films. Never told Big Fred the story. What was the point of work after L'avventura? And let's not forget Il grido. The Scream."

There are tears in his eyes.

"I haven't forgotten," I say. Did a whole chapter on it."

"Vitti did a dub for Il grido. Before they were involved. He hears the voice and that's it. Never got over her."

"Some asshole," I say, "big shot film commentator, called her horse-faced."

"Cocksucker!"

"Several senses of the word, Mr. Chairman."

"Nice, Morelli: You're improving, even as we speak."

"You never read my dissertation?"

"I took it in."

"You didn't interview me, either."

He leans in, he whispers: "I took you in."

◆ ◆ ◆

The self-regarding neogothic buildings of the college cling to a steep hill-side at the western outskirts of the small city of Stormbridge. The largest belongs to central administration; the smallest to the library. The sole eye-catcher, a uniquely ill-formed structure, hosts the airless gymnasium and a nondenominational chapel which is flanked on one side by the Office of Psychological Options and, on the other, by a beer-only bar friendly to underage freshmen. Film and Video sits just beneath the Provost in administration, where we occupy an entire floor, featuring an exhaustive collection of films and seminar rooms for our use only, heavy with state of the art technology. Most of the faculty commute two or three days a week from Danbury, Waterbury, Hartford, New Haven and even Manhattan (the Provost via helicopter). Jack and I chose to live undercover in Stormbridge proper, whose population still bears a significant number of citizens of Italian-American descent. As Jack put it, we were drawn to Stormbridge's Italian-American precincts because we needed serious practice if we had any hope of moving from ex to "actual-full-time-wops."

Stormbridge's heroic Italian immigrants have, of course, all long gone to their reward and their children — those still alive — are in their eighties and nineties. The grandchildren of the first generation — those in Jack's age category — have mostly left home. Many of them are also dead. Those who stayed run their parents' small businesses — restaurants, bakeries, pizzerias, auto repair garages, plumbing and electrical concerns and one floral shop whose owner is said to be Stormbridge's only homosexual, who was, nevertheless, getting plenty. In Stormbridge. The great grandchildren of the immigrants, they're in my age category, bear names like Tiffany, Lindsay, Britney, Evan, and Barry — like me, newly baked white bread of the fourth generation. All the Tiffanys and Evans who'd fled Stormbridge for many distant cities would find that those nice little businesses had been lovingly willed to them, but they would not come back to run them. They would rush out of Stormbridge, rush, within an hour of watching their remaining parent's coffin shoved rudely, with an awful grinding racket, into a mausoleum wall.

It was to Rintrona's Bakery and Café that I carried my notebooks and dissertation every morning at 7:00, opening time, to work until noon, and to confront the final rewrite that would turn the dissertation into an accessible manuscript worthy of publication by a major press. The lingering aroma of the previous night's baking was deeply tranquilizing — almost as comforting as the owner, Cliff Rintrona, who had little to do after his supply trucks left the premises at 6:30 except to sink into the usual bleak moods that he combatted daily by coming to my table on the average of once every hour. He liked my company. He brightened. Those distractions — several minutes each in duration — refreshed me for what I needed to believe were the deeper reaching efforts to refine my argument and make my style less sinful.

When the University of Chicago Press accepted the manuscript, I decided to dedicate it, secretly, to Cliff. The plan: bring a finished copy of the book to the bakery at my usual time and surprise him. Cliff wouldn't know the ways of books. I'd subtly nudge him to page through the front matter, slowly — go back a page, Cliff — until he came upon it: To Cliff Rintrona, One of Nature's Last Good Men. I imagine him saying, Is nature an atheistical professor's way of referring to God? Hank, there's lots of good ones out there. You think too much of me, kid. Upon receipt of the first copies, I bring one to the bakery where I find Cliff on the floor, unconscious. I call Emergency Medical Services. They arrive within minutes to pronounce him dead.

Cliff is (was) advanced in age, but not in appearance. He stood ramrod straight. Had all of his hair, silver and crew cut, the forearms of a major league home run hitter and — despite those long hours in the bakery — sported a ruddy outdoors complexion. Nevertheless.

I have a habit, in my writing and in everyday life, of getting too far ahead of myself, of racing toward what lies ahead — you know what lies ahead — with open arms racing toward what awaits me with open arms and preternatural confidence. You've barely met Cliff — who plays a key role in my story — and I've already killed him off. You ask me, What time is it? I glance at my watch and observe that it's 10:31. I respond, It's almost eleven.

"Cliff" wasn't his name. He invented it as a survival strategy after his given name was made fun of by classmates. One day, so the story goes, when he was seven and on the way to school, he decides he can't take the humiliation anymore and sits down on a curb and cries. I'm not going to school! I'm running away! His brother, Angelo, eighteen years old, happens by and tries to console him. What's the matter, Dom? What's wrong with little Domenico? Domenico cries harder and punches Angelo, you bitchin' bastard! I don't want to be Domenico no more! Don't call me Domenico no more! Okay brother, don't hurt me, says Angelo, from now on your name is Clifford. That's what you write on your school papers. When the teacher asks what's going on, you say your parents changed your name because they wanted you to be a real American. Domenico says, Ang, I will write Clifford, but I ain't sayin' Clifford. I'm saying Cliff! Why, Ang asks, can't you call yourself Clifford? I'm not telling you, Ang. Clifford is high class, kid. A name like that goes to Yale. I like the one I made up better. But why? Because you didn't make it up: I did.

Then Cliff and Angelo begin to dance, circling each other like two boxers sparring, unleashing lethal shadow left-right combinations to each other's head and torso. Angelo mock-crumples to the pavement. Struggles to get up, but can't make it to his feet before the count of ten as little Cliff raises his arms in triumph. From the pavement, Angelo cheers. Never again, Cliff said, would they be so happy.

Cliff told me that story after we'd known each other for about two weeks — when he was bringing me every morning breakfast that he cooked up in the back kitchen. He wouldn't let me pay. I said, Come on Cliff, I should pay. Come on. Cliff's response, There's no point in that. What's the point in that? Then he said, Remember the story I told you about me and Angelo? I didn't have the heart to say to him — he was eighty-one years old — that he'd told me the story three days before. Then he said, When Angelo was twenty-one, he was murdered.

◆ ◆ ◆

THE SEMINAR

The long rectangular table around which they sit is too big for the small, windowless room. To move around it when entering or leaving, the seminarians must walk sideways, in the mode of the crab, or posterior first, in the mode of the backward devils. The walls, painted dead white, are barren except for a clock affixed to the wall behind the chair where the rookie professor has chosen, thoughtlessly, to sit. A clock four feet directly above his head. A rookie's mistake, which will cause serious irritation. At times, it will make him seethe. Attached to the wall opposite the professor, who sits alone at one of the shorter sides of the rectangle, a screen for the viewing of film clips.

Eight students, Jack Del Piero, the woman who calls herself Nadia De Simoni, but whose true surname remains unknown, even to Jack, and the teacher whose syllabus identifies him as H.L.R. Morelli. Seven students come bearing sleek laptops and the eighth — New England's NCAA Division II champion wrestler in the 184 pound category — brings nothing but an unnerving combination of ease and intensity. Across from the wrestler and within touching distance of Morelli, the long-legged blond knockout Nadia, who embodies a level of cool Nordic beauty that drives away all men like Hank (they are numberless) who would like to touch her, but whose self-confidence is not robust. That gloom-ridden figure beside her is heavier than the wiry phenomenon of his famous twenties: Jack Del Piero is now puffy-eyed, bald domed, modestly paunched, but sturdy and much stronger looking, thanks to his weight lifting regimen. As Nadia likes to say, "Jack is so fit."

Though rare, and generally inappropriate, for faculty to audit a colleague's class — outrageously so, in this instance — the untenured rookie can hardly refuse his chairman, who'll be the chief determinate of his professional fate. Del Piero didn't wish to be present, he explained, in order to "put your balls in a vise." He was simply drawn irresistibly to the mystery of the announced topic. Mystery enhanced by their conversation of the week before at the Provost's party. Hank wanted, and needed, to accept Del Piero at his word. Nevertheless, he felt — at the very thought of Jack's impending presence — painful pressure about the gonads.

By design, Professor Morelli is the last to enter the classroom — a long blazing silk scarf floating behind: the single theatrical gesture of a life thus far without drama. (The longed for drama.) A scarf on September 1, at Fahrenheit 80°. He says, "Good afternoon" and Nadia, on whom he's not laid eyes until this moment, replies, thrillingly, "Hello, Hank." Jack nods, gives a little wave. The wrestler says, "Hey there," giving the thumbs up sign. The others sit shocked in silence by the appearance of this new professor in a form-fitting, custom-tailored Italian suit: six foot four, dark wavy hair (think matinee idols of the 1940s and 50s), blue-eyes, well built, with head-turning handsomeness of which he has no awareness. His eyes are often averted and he's self-conscious in the manner of those (especially women) whose imperial height is acquired too soon, when all the little playmates have yet to achieve their growth. From the age of thirteen, until his death in old age, Morelli wants to be shorter.

He calls the role. They respond vocally with the exception of the one who raises his hand. This is Hector Moreno, laptopper #7. A name, a response, then a five second stare at the responder, in a desperate effort to link name and face and lock it into memory. (He would rarely succeed.)

The professor speaks again: "Welcome to Film Studies, 150" and before he can say another word one of the laptoppers who's been checking his e-mail says, "You mean this isn't Econ. 100, section 18?" Morelli says, "You're welcome to stay, sir." The student says, "What's the subject here?" Morelli intones, "The Crisis of Temporality in the Cinema of Michelangelo Antonioni." The student says, "I didn't know that Michelangelo made movies." One of the laptoppers says, "Lame, Harold." In a tone both erotic and ominous, Nadia says, "You want to see a movie? I'll show you a movie." The kid hurries out.

Before Morelli on the table not a set of notes but the 827-page manuscript of his dissertation and the requisite bottle of designer water. The plan is to conduct the seminar as a blend of lecture, he'll read from the manuscript, and Socratic dialogue. Should there be no dialogue, should his read remarks be met with silence, and he have to face the prospect of going it alone for three hours, then he would lecture formally. (Let 'em sit there in silence. I'll read every goddamn written word even if it takes the entire semester.) The dissertation represented his precise thinking, so why shouldn't he deliver it, word for word? The tuition was steep at Western Connecticut, so why not give them his best, word for word? It was, after all, the Oxford way.

He says, "Shall we begin?"

Nadia says, "Why do you ask?"

Jack says, "He didn't."

"I beg your pardon, Jack, but he most certainly did," crossing her legs. Hiked up skirt.

Beads of sweat on Hank's forehead.

"Ice-breaker, baby, empty rhetorical question," Jack replies.

She touches Hank's elbow and says, "Quick, professor, fill me up."

With the exception of the wrestler, all student jaws drop.

"To begin at the beginning, then, let us briefly consider our title. The Crisis of Temporality in the Cinema of Michelangelo Antonioni."

"Your title," Jack says. "It's all yours."

"Let us, then, in any event, consider it. Assuming" (here hoping for a laugh) "the clarity of 'the,' 'of', and 'in'" — no reaction — "and assuming in addition that we all know who I refer to when I say Michelangelo Antonioni" — the wrestler nods, the laptoppers glaze over in stupefaction — "let us, then, proceed to the problematics of 'cinema,' 'temporality,' and 'crisis,' in that order, if you will. If I may."

The wrestler says, "Thy will be done."

The laptoppers smile benignly.

Morelli believes that he's winging it beautifully, actually believes that he's speaking naturally, that he can actually teach, rather than read a lecture, with maybe minimal attention to his manuscript. That powerhouse wrestler is on his side, isn't he?

Out of nowhere, fear, like a hammer, slams into his back. He wants to speak off the cuff about the concept of crisis, but can't, because he's having one. He begins turning the front pages of his manuscript until he gets to the introductory chapter: "Foundational Terms and Concepts."

He'll not read. He wants to wing it again. He'll try. With an exuberantly irrelevant gesture, he says, "Why 'cinema' rather than 'films' or 'movies'? 'Movies' are the Hollywood thing for mass consumption. Conventional pap. Escapist crap. 'Film'? The preferred word of American academics who wish to put distance between themselves and the odor of crap. Crap now pleasurably inhaled all over the world. 'Cinema' is European. Rings pretentiously to the American ear. Pompous. Pomposo! Good. I say good. Calls attention to something different, which we don't want to know about."

The wrestler says, "Kindly define 'we.'"

"World-wide crap inhalers."

The wrestler asks, "People in this room?"

"We shall see."

Laptopper #1: "Sir, what is it that we don't want to know?"

Laptopper #2: "That's what we're here for, Ralph."

Laptopper #1, who has a crush on laptopper #2: "Harriet, do you have to take that tone with me?"

Laptopper #3: "Sir, time will tell what we're here for, am I right?"

"'Time' will not tell. The word is temporality. Why 'temporality' and not 'time'? Why 'temporality' and not 'time'? Because 'time' can't drive home the needed point. 'Time,' as a word, *is* dead."

The wrestler says, "That's why we prefer it."

"Absolutely, Cameron. What time shall we meet for drinks, and so forth."

Nadia says, "Soon, I trust."

Student laughter — excluding the wrestler.

Hank: "'Time' lies. Puts us to sleep. Which is the whole point of saying 'time'. I'll see you a week from tomorrow, and so forth. Slumber. We don't say, What temporality is it, dear? Did you have a nice temporality, dear?"

Jack: "This temporality, I'm on top, dear."

Very long silence.

Hank resumes: "'Temporality' is intimately linked to Antonioni's 'cinema,' the aesthetic habitation of temporality. 'Temporality,' like 'cinema,' is poison poured into the American ear. Calls attention to the ground of all fear — life on this shattered earth, with no exit down the abyss. Down the hole of self. Temporality. Antonioni's cinema rubs our noses in it."

"As in shit," Jack asks?

"As in irredeemable death," Hank replies. "Yes."

"Now it's clear," Jack says.

"About temporality versus time," Hank responds?

"No," Jack says. "Now I'm convinced I was smart to push for your appointment with the Provost."

The wrestler nods.

Professor Morelli reads stiffly from a note he's scribbled on the title page of his manuscript: "Let us now repair to our unisex restroom. You may take ten minutes. Thank you so much." When they return, Hank looks pale, stricken. He has no choice. He must read:

"Crisis. For whom? For Antonioni's characters? One finds most of them aswim in the sea of banality, saying crisis so frequently, so lightly, in fogs of unmeaning. The crisis, they say, of a bad hair day, when a massive high pressure system squats over the throne of northern Italy. For such characters, one has no interest except in so far as they hurl — they hurl into highest relief those afflicted at the so-called core of so-called self. One thinks of that fatal figure of crisis, Monica Vitti (Monica!). But a crisis too for Antonioni himself because the world of his cinema is nothing other than this auteur's expressive exfoliation, a sickly leafing out from the moribund tree of himself, of what one might call his majorly fucked up, if not fucked over, consciousness. Let us be clear. The crisis of which one here speaks is not a crisis for Antonioni. More rigorously, one must say, this crisis *is* Antonioni, that looming figure of modern-man-as-crisis. Shall we say a crisis for his audience? For us? Let us say it, in so far as we dare allow ourselves to be vulnerable, in wide open vulnerability, spreading the moist inner thighs of our closed subjectivity in anticipation of Antonionian entry.

"Crisis, to place our big hermeneutical feet firmly on familiar, though uncanny, ground, is pathological: That point in the progress of the disease of our being-in-the-world when important change takes place, heralding, for better or for worse, the turning point of the spirit's recuperation, or its death. Can there be health of and in crisis itself? A condition not to be overcome but to be lived in? A sprezzatura of crisis? A Fred Astaire-like dancing on the sharp-pointed pivot of critical change? A joy and ecstasy of crisis? At long last, a tranquility of crisis? Even, mon Dieu! a hugging of the big bad grizzly of crisis, who would tear off in delight large chunks of our yummy ass?"

He stops, takes a long swig on his bottle, then with downcast eyes says, "Questions, comments, counterclaims, outraged diatribes?"

Jack says, "I believe rewriting is taking place."

Nadia says, "I believe I'm being rewritten."

The wrestler asks if in scholarly work "the f-word" is common and Morelli replies, "It occurs."

The wrestler says, "Are you saying Antonioni created fucked-up films because he was himself fucked-up? If so, aren't you committing a version of the genetic fallacy? Do you consider fucked-up an honorific term, in which case are you praising him just because he is fucked-up? No disrespect, sir, but you seem awfully young to be infected with the countercultural values of the 1960s."

Hank responds, "I'm from Chicago."

Laptopper #1 says, "Speaking of counterculture, is everybody aware that's a cool brand of coffee?"

Laptopper #2: "Your point, Ralph?"

Laptopper #1: "My point, Harriet, as if you didn't know, is context. Cultural context. Resonance, Harriet."

Laptopper #3: "All those questions you posed, are you going to answer them before the midterm exam?"

"No."

Laptopper #3: "Before the final?"

"No."

Laptopper #3: "Uh . . . who is Fred Adare? At least give us that."

Laptopper #4: "Why a grizzly? Why not a gorilla? I'm coming from animal rights."

Hank: "I'm coming from fatigue."

The wrestler: "Whether or not you ever answer the questions you posed, sir, do you really think they're relevant to Antonioni's depressing cinema? An ecstasy of crisis?"

"No comment."

"Nice move, Morelli!" Jack says. "Nice move."

Nadia: "I love the way you pronounced sprezzatura. How did it feel on the tongue? Feel good?"

Professor Morelli: "Afraid I'm not well. I must arise and go now."

"See you same time next week?" says the wrestler.

Laptopper #5: "Time is of the clock."

Laptopper #6: "The clock can't measure temporality. Temporality is what is endured, behind the thick walls and locked door of the self, waiting for the end."

Professor Morelli, deeply happy, actually looks at #5 and #6: "Our lesson has perhaps been a success."

The wrestler: "Next week, then?"

Professor Morelli: "Anything is possible."

Laptopper #7, who has not, and will never speak, types a note: "Temporality is time that does not pass. Time that does not pass is not to be confused with eternity. It's still (pun?) time."

Out of respect, all remain seated while Morelli struggles — sideways, backwards — to the door. He opens it, hesitates at the threshold, then with a whirl turns to the class — his scarf whipping behind. He holds up and shakes a page of his manuscript. "Temporality?" he says. "I give it to you from the Old Norse, 'thick' and 'swollen' — the tumescence of time. And from the

Latin, 'thin' — the anorexia of time. Check this out: From the Old Lithuanian, 'stretch,' — the limousine of time. Take the road of contradiction — it will lead you, I promise, to the palace of wisdom."

That night, late, watching a ball game in extra innings, Morelli mutes the sound — so much the better to hear the stranger's constructed voice looping in his head. It's an embarrassing voice that doesn't speak, it intones . . . expressive exfoliation . . . temporality . . . sprezzatura . . . hermeneutical . . . mon Dieu . . . pomposo . . . pomposo . . . pomposo. . . .

6 ◆ Desiring Claudia Cardinale

EDITOR'S NOTE
The Jack Del Piero we meet here is a younger version of the character who appears in "The Rookie Professor." The action takes place several years before that section.

FROM THE ITALIAN ACTRESS (2010)

It was there, in Volterra, two years ago, that I found them: the fantastically named Sigismondo Malatesta and his companion of a thousand devious allures, who called herself Isotta degli Atti. It was in Volterra — Tuscany's most forbidding walled city of stone — at an obscure festival — the only kind that invites me now. In that harsh place, where I won no prize for continuing achievement in video, or any other prize, at the villa of an aging Italian film star (female, divorced, rich, beautiful still, and available) who said, it was Claudia, actually Claudia, and she said — violent thunder and lightning breaking over the mountains, driving the guests from her garden and leaving the two of us standing alone and too close in sudden dark, awaiting rain — and Claudia at that moment said in her fatal, raucous voice, "Jack, you cannot win a prize because you are in your own self the prize. Am I old enough to be your mother? Sì, certo! Do we care? Are you afraid? Speak to me. Why don't you speak?" I laughed in a certain way, because I could not speak. I finally summoned words. I said, stupidly, "Thank you, Claudia" and she replied, "Is that what you want to do, Jack? To thank me? What have I given?"

In her vicinity, I tended to shortness of breath. I thought of this woman as I thought of the work I hadn't been doing for so long and the work I wanted yet to do: it's not going to happen, because passion is a word in a language I had long since ceased to understand, if ever I did. (Do I care that she is old enough to be my mother? I have yet to decide.)

My name is Jack Del Piero, former avant-garde videographer, long detached — without regret — from my Italian-American origins. If you wish, you may gloss "former avant-garde" as "last week's wilted salad," or — should you be of brutal disposition — call me "garbage," on the menu still and a favorite with those of nostalgic appetite. I'm also a periodic stutterer who would sing with all the notes connected, as in a single breath, but fluency is a river

I'll not swim in: better to write than to talk.

Twenty years ago, my silent videos won special prizes at Taormina and Venice for "their radical experiments in pornography and the beauty of their images." Osservatore Romano pronounced my soul an abomination. "His actors," wrote the reviewer for Le Monde, "are at all times fully clothed. Never do they touch, one another, or themselves, but the erotic charge is unbearable. What exactly is done in Mr. Del Piero's disturbing art is unspeakable in public print, even in Paris."

In the mirror of my videos I banish disaster; I banish myself. There, and nowhere else, I find myself a figure of surpassing grace and savage wit, handsome even; my father's son at last. But at the time I met her — Claudia — I hadn't made a video in twenty years; I'd reverted to being inescapable Jack Del Piero.

They invited me to Volterra (at Claudia's urging, she revealed much later) for the same reason I was invited to all the marginal festivals: As an ironic example for the idealistic young — I mean the attractive, the fresh-faced, the energetic, the goddamn young — a blasted figure of purity and poverty I am, out of the past, salt and pepper hair to the shoulders, lean and hard at 48 (two years ago: I grow old), and apparently not unappealing, if I can trust Claudia. I suppose I mean, see myself through her eyes, which I cannot.

In Volterra, I served as bitter inspiration for the up and comers who'd one day receive, perhaps they'd receive, once or twice, no more than that, glancing — barely glancing — notice at festivals more questionable even than the one at Volterra and who would attempt to assuage themselves to the grave with my memory, thinking of themselves, absurdly, as artistic kin, as having once made it to my level before disappearing, like me, into romantic obscurity — not able ever to think of themselves truthfully (an infinitely excusable fault) as among the legion of artists who were, from the beginning, forever down, and out of sight, and never romantic.

Meeting me, Malatesta said that night at Claudia's, was like meeting the immensely gifted fifth bassoonist of the London Philharmonic, third cousin of John Lennon, whose name (the fifth bassoonist's) would remain forever on the tip of the tongue, never to be recalled, never to be spoken. "Until now," he said: "and here you are, Jack, face to face in Volterra and they are eager to talk with someone else. They are so embarrassed for you and for themselves, especially for themselves, because they do not wish to be near you, they have no interest, they cannot withstand your putrefying presence and who can blame them? (Though Isotta and I are drawn to it: your putrefaction.) You are the mirror of their future. You are invited here to teach them who they are. Caro mio, I must tell you that Isotta and I have a plan. Without you, we cannot tell our story; the plot fails." Isotta added, "In Rimini, you work as you like, or waste time as you like." Sometime later, I asked Malatesta how many bassoonists were seated in the London Philharmonic. He replied, "Four."

I take late coffee and oranges and too many cornetti (marmalade-infused) on her wind swept veranda, with a view to the walled and towered city, her olive orchard spilling below me silver and green down the hill into the deep-clefted and awful gorge that separates villa and Volterra — a mile across as the crow flies — the city high on its imperious throne of rock. Volterra is medieval old, cold and grim — a uniform world of gray stone — no trees, no flowers, no shrubs, no grass — a paradise of the inorganic, of death — and deeply, deeply comforting to contemplate, the object of this would-be ascetic's desire. In opposition — these were my every morning's choices — there she is, before me in the heated pool, calling out as I meditate on my fiftieth birthday, as I grow fat about the middle in my second year with her, my second year of pregnancy (I am big with Claudia). She, the subversion of my tranquility — my icy dream of Volterra — she, that sumptuous and supple body, brown and naked, afloat in liquid turquoise. "Jack," she says, she laughs, "I like you with your new belly. Tonight I make the ponytail. Now you must for me jump in and join my pleasure. Quick, caro, take off your clothes." The raucous voice says "pleasure," but promises delights not exclusively, or even predominantly, erotic.

She says that she is the solution. She says that we are the story. She says that so-called Sigismondo and Isotta (those appalling mountebanks) are not the story. I tell her that I disagree. I tell her so often, and she replies just as often, and always the same, that it is preferable to choose simplicity: "my bed," she says, "and wild boar steak, the tomatoes heavy from the vine and the basil and the figs, the figs big like pears, I pick them for you, they are warm still, like me, from the sun, and warm more from the hands that pick them. Touch my hand, Jack, before it is too late. Your hands are cold. Jump in and lose your brains."

I did not jump in; I'm not one to jump in. I talked. Even now, with some understanding of who the man is who writes this, as he remembers, I wouldn't change the words that I'd say to her — if I could say them to her now, as I said them then. Words hidden in me, day and night: When I saw you first in "8 1/2,"

Claudia, in white, the day itself a bowl of white, you came gliding over the grass — do you remember? — your smile sailed me in a surround of white sky and I couldn't tell you from the radiance, you were the embodied radiance as you came to Marcello in his fantasy — I was there, I was the unseen fantasist as you descended to minister to the faulty instincts of our manhood. Did the jaded crew prick up its ears and stare?

Later, in that scene in the hotel room, where our desire summoned you in chiaroscuro, you and I and Marcello in salacious complicity to betray the Angel of Mercy, you smoothed the bedsheets, terrifying us in your slip, then turned, lubricious, to the camera's gaze (I was the camera) radiant still but darkly so in the blood light of eros. You came as someone else — who are you really, Claudia? — you came to minister to the needy again, but for a different kind of need. Do you remember?

This is how she responded to my moon-struck rhapsody: First with a kind laugh. Then this: "It is only the light design; it is only the cinematografia; it is only the acting, though it does not please me to call it acting. Because I am in Fellini only a volume of space, like a tree, or chair, but more flexible. Are you hearing me? The films are false. You have the chance to destroy the lies of my mystery. But you make more mystery. In the scenes you talk about I do not speak; I am only a body. But I speak. Who am I really? Before I go to bed or to make love I go to the toilet. Are you understanding me? I am here. Are you here? Come, jump in and I will make you real. I don't tell her that, unlike you, Claudia, Volterra is hard, Volterra repels, — and that's why I'm drawn to it.

I sat on her veranda in all kinds of weather because I believed that the sick improve (I do not say get well) in the open air. I contracted my ills when I left Claudia — not reluctantly — for an extended period, to work in Rimini and to play a considerable role in the plot of Sigismondo and Isotta. The point of Rimini was work: I was working again, I was going to look in the mirror of my new video and pronounce myself the man I wanted to be. These ills of mine, I admit, are in part mental, or — as my father was fond of saying to me in my teen years — "only mental." My father found himself — on occasion — mildly funny, and so did I.

◆ ◆ ◆

Claudia says it's easier to choose life and that only the mad overcome the difficulty of the choice for death. I am not mad, she assures me. She says I am sad (no rhyme in Italian) and must embrace the sadness *con tutta la tua forza* (with all your power). If I do that, then I shall embrace her for our good remaining days on this terrible earth. You desire to embrace me, Jack, though you do not. She insists it's best to choose the easy course because the end will be hard enough and reassures me (reassurance being her most reiterated speech act) that I am safe now. "In my house," Claudia says, "we are not actors; it is not permitted."

I believed it possible that I'd recover; believed this especially when she took me riding in her vintage '65 Mustang, meticulously restored, on narrow roads, top down over hills blanketed with vineyards and a countryside dominated by islands of noble cypresses and the occasional ochre-colored villa. We avoid the obvious: Siena and Florence. We work, but fail to skirt the difficulty between us as we take the narrowest of side roads, lanes really — the vegetation and overhanging trees virtually closing off the passage in places, brushing the sides of the car — where we are at last free of careening Italian motorcyclists. We stop here and there awhile in forgotten villages — no tourists, no art treasure — villages of a single café on a desolate little piazza where we take a macchiato and sweet around eleven and, at four, a small sandwich of salami and provolone, with Campari on the rocks, at a table on the piazza, under a canopy, during sudden showers interrupted by sudden shafts of sun, the light brilliant on the ruined façade across the way. We take our pleasure in the food and drink and each other: on this latter, she vocally, me in silence.

I tell her she is the sudden shaft of sunlight, I the more than intermittent shower, the too often all day downpour, and she replies, "Yes, we go together like prosciutto and cold melon." Then one time I blurt it out, I say, "Let's tell the truth, Claudia, I've been living with you for two years, more or less, and we have yet to make love. I point to the ruined façade and say, I am that ruined façade." She says, "Not in my house, this ruined façade; you make too much drama." She says, "Anticipation is good." (Sigismondo's favorite line.)

Apropos of nothing, I tell her that my parents cared dearly for me, my childhood was not tragic, but they cared for one another even more, perhaps too much more and for this sin of passion they carried guilt for me and self-loathing, they carried these things like old broken down pack horses dying of thirst in the desert and needing the mercy of a sudden bullet in the brain. She says, "Today you talk pretty again like the writers I do not read." I tell her that my mother got what she needed: a massive coronary, out of the blue — she who had no family history of such problems hit the floor like a ton of bricks. My father also got what he wanted: the flair of a theatrical big finish: Wagnerian

Liebestod. Claudia says we will not endure such problems, because she is too old to give birth "and if you wait much longer to make love to me I will be under the earth. No children, no guilt, no loathing of ourselves, but the sadness, of course. It is possible a big heart attack. Why not? But Wagner? No Wagner in my house and the only Verdi we are permitting is *Falstaff.* Because it is better to be *buffoni,* the two of us, but especially you, Signor Melodrama. And the Beatles, *sì*: I love you yeah yeah yeah." (I fail to withhold a grin.)

I say, "I'm going to do it, I'm going to edit the Rimini video." She says, "In my house?" "I'll go public with this horror," I say, "I'm coming back strong at Taormina, I'll take it all the way to Cannes." She says, "If you wish; I do not wish. Do you wish, Jack, in your secret heart?" I say, "I don't know. Only The Shadow knows." "In my house," she laughs, she says, "shadows are not permitted."

So it goes: touring the Tuscan hills, chatting in lonely cafés. Or much reading (me) and much gardening (she). Claudia reads little. She keeps house, not because she doesn't want to spend for help but because she likes it. Soccer is an addiction: she is an Italian. She says that when Roberto Baggio missed the penalty kick in overtime at the World Cup she became "scarred for life." She watches the soccer channels in the afternoon and is teaching me to understand this beautiful game, beautiful (like Claudia) even when I do not understand. These are our days. Our nights: We cook together. She's good, but soon, she says, I'll be better. And it's probably true. I have the touch, but not the experience. Or the will. We go to bed in separate rooms, without submerged rancor. There is no rancor.

After two years I'm making some progress: I'm almost used to looking at her; I share a villa with one of the world's most stunning women and I'm possibly on the blessed road to ordinariness. Getting over her looks is not really the problem. (Well, somewhat of a problem.) It's getting over the way she takes me in; the obvious (even to me) pleasure she takes in my company (even my long silences). From the beginning she's behaved as if we've known each other forever, and it's no act: "Not in *casa mia,* although you, Jack, sometimes make operas out of yourself." It's the quality of her attention and it's difficult, maybe impossible, for me to accept that I could be the object of that gaze, that she is not suffering from some temporary hallucination which, once it passes — you complete the thought. When I sense that my capitulation is near, I tell her that I am my father's son. This is my final line of defense. I remind her of how he went out, that passion is the royal road to self-destruction. She only says, "What was your father's name? It was Frank, yes? Is your name Frank? Are you changing your name to Frank? No? Why not? I am closing the case. Basta, Jack." (A week ago, I touched held her hand.)

Claudia is candid, improbably unaware of her charm, but not unaware, how could she be? of her beauty: "I am beautiful, they say, but what can it matter when we eat breakfast together with bad breath after 2,000 days?" Only the truly unaffected can smile as she does. Above all, she is unpredictably exciting. On that first night in Volterra she brushed aside my comments about her films, took my hand and led me to the vast garage to show me an ancient Mercedes engine, laid out in what seemed to me, but not to her, a chaos of pieces, small and large, on a grease-stained floor. With the enthusiasm of a teenage boy, she was learning automechanics from a forbidding technical manual, also grease-stained: the kind of book, she said, that she enjoyed. The following morning — that is, the morning after the first of many chaste nights at the villa — she took me to an outdoor market and pointed out that all the customers were women because women must do these things, but she, who has many euros to hire servants, goes to market twice a week because the sight of fresh produce and the odor of fresh bread lifts the fallen flesh — this said with a frank glance downward to her wondrous chest. It pleases her to tell me at the fish market that her brother, professor of cinema in Palermo, upon hearing of her interest many years ago in my infamous videos, had summarized for her the ideas of a still landmark study of my importance to the field, the international bestseller *The Pornographics of Everyday Life: Notes on the Structure of Postmodern Beauty*. It was fortunate that Renato had explained this difficult thinking (which drew her closer to the idea of me before we met — closer, she said, than even these excellent stinks of fish) because she herself was not capable of reading such a book. She said that many "bombs of sex" from the movies, "like poor Marilyn," wish to be valued for their minds, that she had been one of those big bombs, she too had a mind, but it was not a mind in the sense that Renato and the other bombs meant this word of the intellectual class. She said that if we should value each other, it would be for everything we absorbed from "the eyes, the ears, the hands and the mouth, especially the tongue, because this is how healthy people find the spirit and the mind, there is no other way, *caro mio,* I do not want to be loved for my so-called mind alone."

When Claudia speaks, I am almost composed. (Yesterday, I touched her shoulder.)

◆ ◆ ◆

I treat her to my reflections on minor Italian cities. I say, "Maybe I'll do a career change and become a travel writer."

She replies, "Can you do this and not leave Volterra again?"

I tell her that tourists demand Florence, Siena, and the territory between — "the Chianti region, where hills and cozy valleys are fluently intertwined — like fortunate lovers," I say, tactlessly; "where you become the measure of an intimate world, the vital center of space and time. Where you feel safe."

"Can you touch me now? In my vital center? I want to feel safe."

"In Volterra, the land falls disastrously away, undermined by obscure forces that create a desolate terrain of cliffs. On the long approach to the city, as you traverse the way to the top, all is steeply eroded: in Spring not a wild flower blooms."

"This is not true," Claudia says. "I have seen two wild flowers."

"The view from outside Volterra's walls is of five disturbing valleys, without end. Mist blurs the outlines of all objects — form deteriorates into formlessness, the insecure. You are not the center; there is no center; you feel an encroaching terror."

"But what do you truly fear? I do not believe that it can be Volterra. Tesoro, I, also, have fear, but not of Volterra."

"With the exception of one building, Rimini is of no interest. For the thousands who in summer invade from Germany and the Scandinavian countries, touring and gazing is never the object. They don't come because they recall Rimini as the city of Fellini's birth and the subject of two of his films. They have heard the name Fellini, but have not seen the films. Many, in fact, are no doubt of the assured opinion that Fellini is a variety of pasta, short and wide."

"When you have truly recovered from your illness, you will be kinder and not make such cruel jokes. You will not fear to be kind."

"Nor do those northern invaders, dear Claudia, come in the hot months because they remember and are drawn by the singular name of Rimini's legendary and lethal ruling family — Malatesta, the name that conjured fear and hatred in the thirteenth, the fourteenth, the fifteenth centuries. They have no need, as I did, to stalk narrow, cobbled streets — seeking contact where once he, Sigismondo, strolled in outrageous arrogance — he, the most shocking of Malatesta scions, the original Sigismondo, Renaissance soldier of fortune, and bloody visionary who caused the Tempio Malatestiano to be erected as a monument to himself and his passion for Isotta degli Atti, the third wife. He loved her to distraction."

"Maybe it made him happy to be distracted."

"He invited Piero della Francesca to Rimini to live and paint in his castle and diddle his servants of both sexes, if he so wished. I was seeking contact with this Sigismondo, said to have murdered his first two wives in order to clear the path for Isotta, to whom he'd lost himself. Sometimes, he'd written to her, a few weeks before his death, with these Popes and Cardinals it is required that with my knife I go in."

"I think you care for this dead man. Are you in love?"

"They come to Rimini for the sun, the beaches of white sand, the warm and murky Adriatic."

"Are you in love?"

"They come in hopes of an unforgettable encounter with an astonishing (if unemployed) Italian, and they are not denied."

"I am an unemployed Italian — formerly astonishing."

"In winter, Rimini is a ghost town — battered by gale-force winds off the sea, fog-enshrouded, cold and damp. Especially in winter, I found Rimini irresistible."

After I've finished treating her to my dyspeptic ruminations, Claudia responds, fiercely, "Is it possible that you are writing a travel book for malcontents? Why do you make these comparisons? Why is it necessary to make comparisons of these places, if you are truly content to be living where you are, with me, in Volterra, which you say that you prefer? If you so much prefer it to be here, near my body — this is my body, Jack — why must you say it so much that it is better for you to be here, with me? Your color is not so good."

Those two in Rimini called regularly after I met them in Volterra — I refused their invitation many times, but finally, after three months with Claudia, in early December, I accepted "to make," as they put it, "something very rare." When I informed her that I'd be leaving for Rimini, for how long I didn't know, just as I didn't know if I'd ever be back, she said, "Do you know who these people are?" "Yes, I think they're frauds." "No, Jack, they are only actors." I said, "I'm going anyway." For reply, she made a large gesture — comic, very Italian, and untranslatable. Had she repeated it, I might never have left.

◆ ◆ ◆

I know what my father would have said. Because hadn't he — chaired professor of Extreme Aesthetics at Princeton — already said it, memorably, many years before, in a scholarly journal? "We cannot physically desire a woman whom we perceive and contemplate as beautiful. If we attempt to make love to her, we fail, even if she comes eagerly to us in her naked glory. The idea of erotic love with a woman of beauty presents itself as an absurdity, as if we had been asked to pole vault over Mount Everest. I submit that the beautiful woman, qua beautiful woman, has never been made love to, not once, because, truly perceived and contemplated, beauty kills desire: it paralyzes the will and awakens us to the thought of soothing death."

Had my father's argument ended there, it wouldn't have stirred offended commentary. The "argument qua argument," as one of his condescending fellow philosophers put it, "amounts to a mildly provocative extension of Immanuel Kant and other ascetics of beauty." But in violation of academic protocols, my father insisted on inserting — in the words of one of his detractors — "the slovenly empirical, the shamelessly personal": a revelation that stunned the entire discipline. "My ceaseless desire for my wife," he wrote, "was ignited only after a lengthy spell of chastity, in the early years of our marriage — when the repetitious realities of domestic life had thoroughly worked their disenchanting and banalizing effects on her numinous beauty. Our first sexual contact — how good it was! — followed close upon her first thunderous seizure by flatulence. It was then that I embraced not only my wife but also her wisdom. She'd said, during the long dry spell, 'If beauty lies in the eye of the beholder, then I hope to fill your senses, periodically, with my various corruptions. Darling, you simply cannot fuck an angel, qua angel.'"

Jack, he'd have said, forget the films and photos and attend to Claudia on her sick bed, crawl right in there with her; kiss her before she's brushed her teeth in the morning; request, and pray to be granted, permission to accompany her to the toilet. Then be prepared, if you dare to do these things, for the onset of fierce desire. Have the courage to be human and you'll find her the entirely desirable, if you love.

It was, of course, my father who introduced me to Claudia's great early films, screening them for me many times in my teen years, in order to guide me — deviously, according to his ironic method — but always, I must believe, with my best interests at heart — onto the hard path of my humanization, the path which in his case led to suicide. I was enthralled. I bought the tapes, then the DVDs; when broke, in my early twenties, and working at a video rental store, I skimmed the till for my needs: I bought a sixteen millimeter copy of "8 ½"; I bought the two books of photos, long out of print, published only in Italy, for steep prices; I instructed a rare book dealer to locate and purchase, no matter the price, a pristine copy — I insisted on pristine — only a pristine copy would satisfy me — of the May 1961 issue of Esquire magazine — I was five at the time of its publication — the issue which contained her most ravishing photo, though I, as Daddy would have predicted, was neither ravished or wished to ravish. Instead, I hid her away in the museum — the mausoleum (that's better) of my mind, where I viewed and viewed again, times without number, her lonely image in melancholy space. I was with her there — in melancholy space — released, like her, from this world's contingencies and desires, living inside Claudia's secreted images, where we felt ourselves trying to elude the grip of nature's vicious plot.

Quickly it became vocation and avocation to nourish and indulge my intimate friend — melancholy — a gift (from whom?) that baptized me for art and formed the secret ground beneath my prize-winning videos. Claudia's films and photos belonged to a world I could not have experienced, but nevertheless had invented as memory. As if I had once, with her, been there, had always been there with her. As if it had all, inevitably and deliciously, slipped away from us, except for the retained images — traces of a bygone world, which I cherished more than present life itself.

My appearances at Italian film festivals were occasions to bring her image closer, endow it with local time and habitation. I thought of her as late afternoon light in certain Italian cities (so many) bleeding color; as changing tones of color in changing light (so many tones); as my lonesome impressions, gathered from deserted Italian streets, in autumn and winter, when the tourists have departed, and their loitering consorts, also departed, and gusts of rain swept the streets clean for me, the lone wanderer walking to no end. Most of all, she was the elongated beauty — have you seen Claudia's elegant neck? — of a piazza in Ortigia, at dusk, when the lights of ancient buildings come on to bury the dying light of day and a young girl plays alone a fantasy game of soccer — the booted white ball catching soft light while she sings out Calcio! Mamma! Calcio! In those Italian moments, in those Italian places, I made memories of the present. In Volterra, to shield myself from the presence and present time of Claudia was my exacting vocation. To convert desire to memory was my master strategy, when desire was not, itself, already memory.

I know now why the original Sigismondo, whose streets in Rimini I walked, whose air I believed I'd breathed, whose death room in the Castle — so he named it, camera *della morta,* while he and Isotta lived there in the flush of hot youth — I envisioned myself asleep in that death room, deeply, restfully, where she and he had died — I understood why this intrepid man of action, in his sonnets for the living Isotta, needed to imagine her — make her an image, an untouchable work of art. The image is cold. He imagined her stone cold dead. Presented her the poems as his passion's best gift. I didn't know the body of the beloved — Claudia's body — but I knew intimately what Sigismondo knew, knew it well on the day I came back to her from Rimini, a year after the day we met.

7 ◆ SHOOTING SADDAM

As a young photographer, Ruth Cohen captures indelible images of Castro's Havana during the Cuban Missile Crisis. She's invited to a BBQ by the Kennedys where it's rumored she has a tryst with John F. Kennedy. Overwhelmed by the emotional toll of her Cuban adventure and her newfound notoriety, she drops out of the public eye. The novel begins in 2002 with the reclusive Ruth living in upstate New York with obscure novelist Thomas Lucchesi, author of The Prostate Dialogues. *Ruth is lured out of retirement by an assignment from* The New Yorker *to photograph Saddam Hussein during the run-up to the second Gulf War. This section starts with Ruth and Lucchesi arriving in Baghdad. It alternates between an account of their experience in Iraq and Ruth's life alone in upstate New York afterwards. In Ruth's memories of their time in Iraq, Lucchesi's voice sometimes infects and takes over her consciousness.*

FROM THE BOOK OF RUTH (2005)

There he is at last, bemedaled and beribboned in military dress — the grimly confident warrior, Saddam Hussein. There again, earnest and open-faced in traditional head dress and robe of the countryside — Saddam Hussein, peasant-farmer. And over there, in chest-hair baring white sports shirt, white ducks and sunglasses, rakish, deeply tanned at the wheel of his fabulous yacht — the movie star, the secret crush of every Baathist (men and women alike), Saddam of the killer smile.

In this windowless reception hall at Saddam International — where disembarked passengers contemplate their fate at the crisis of passport control — all is awash in dead light, with the exception of the brilliantly illuminated, 20 by 16 foot four-color posters of the Great Exception Himself, who shall not be underlit. Moving roughly among the passengers, numerous burly-bodied men in black leather jackets — mustachioed in the style of Saddam — talk furtively into their lapels.

A jacket approaches the two bedraggled Americans: "Your passport, vaya con Dios." A glance. "I keep passports for control, no problem, just to control you. I am Mahmood al-Sayyid, your facilitator. May Allah spare you, Señor and Señora! How horrible you look!"

Lucchesi says, "Mahmood, I must inform you that we are not fucking Spaniards."

Mahmood replies, "I am laughing, okay? Mahmood is a sense of humor. Laughing is permitted."

He opens his jacket to reveal a snub-nosed revolver holstered to his belt. He says, "I am saying this is not a sense of humor."

Ruth says, "I am laughing, okay? Ruth is a sense of humor."

Lucchesi says, "Be careful."

Mahmood caresses the revolver.

Ruth says, "May I borrow that for a moment?"

"My dear friends, no more shitting, I am saying. The shitting has ended. Are you ready for Customs? Because at Customs, you will be tested. At Customs, they will screw Saddam himself."

Stationed along the walls, their AK-47s held jauntily at the hip, and pointed toward the passengers, teenage soldiers — looking for adventure.

◆ ◆ ◆

One year later, Ninth Lake.

She's thinking, It would be a nice thing to have, a dog. Could call him Lucky. Or a cat. A cat might be even nicer, who'd jump up on the table and lie here on these photos spread out before me, so much the better to warm them, though she prefers that they remain as they are, like her drafty mountain cabin on this drizzly November night at 41,° whose stove she refuses to fire up. In panties and bra — cold, wanting to be cold. (Cats are cleaner than dogs.) Photos not of Saddam but of Lucchesi — shot over the years from the platform. Photos of her man of changes, who had no idea she was shooting him. (Cats are aloof.) How hopelessly human these photos are, which is why he would have liked them, as would have the legendary art critic he always sided with when he wanted to tease her — the art critic whose single, pontificating sentence about her "noble reticence" had assured the high place of Cuban Stories in the history of American photography.

Storytelling is her grief — exterminate the impulse. Banish the pictorial. Expunge allusion. Suppress the urge to send messages. Annihilate all context. She would look at the world through the eye of her camera and see no worldly significance, no resonance of life. Look at landscapes, and faces, but see only the lurking beauty of the severest geometry, deprived of the consolations of the curvilinear. Beauty fleshless, absolute.

Ruth Cohen believes that she has totally failed, that these photos mock her desire. Because this is what she sees: Lucchesi stories that only she can tell, if only she'd retrieve the context. She remembers: Rescue me, bonita, from this shit of politics.

They find intense affection painful. When they play, they claw and draw blood, because they can't bear very much attention. Cats. Shedding fur everywhere. She remembers: You'll betray me. After I'm gone, as you did before we met. You'll go to bed with another man. After I'm dead. (These photos, these images of her desire for what is not.) Maybe a dwarf rabbit, because they live in a cage, where their shit is contained. You refuse to give it a name. You pet it, hold it for a while, then put it back in the cage, where it belongs, nameless in its cage, in the spare room. Cats need less affection than dogs. Rabbits less than cats. Rocks need nothing — the rapture of rock. (These photos, this companionable pain.)

She remembers: I'll be back late. Mahmood is taking me to a seedy restaurant on the Tigris. A restaurant with a dirt floor. I'm thinking the experience might jump start my stalled writing. My stalled life. (She hears, in the ear of the mind, my stalled wife.) They club the fish to death with a monkey wrench and grill it before your eyes, guts and all. Or for maximum freshness, they pull it with a long-nosed pliers, live from a tiled tub of water, drive a sharp-pointed skewer down its throat and out its bung-hole — then grill it, writhing, before your eyes. Mazgouf. A Baghdad specialty. Come with me, won't you come? She said she wanted to be alone in their vast, traditional Baghdad house. In the silence of the harem.

I asked Mahmood, How do you say, in Arabic, I like to give my wife head? He said, It is not possible, Mr. Lucchesi, to express, or to perform, such a thought in the Arabic frame of reference. Because such an activity defiles God, who abominates the filth of women. If such words are said in Arabic, they signify that someone has chopped your head from your torso and presented it to your wife as a political statement. This is how we give head in Baghdad.

When I return I'll give you head in the harem. We'll defile the culture. Don't go to sleep before we go to bed.

She spends the night in his cabin. In his narrow bed. The next morning, returns to find her cabin ransacked — a window smashed, the mattress up-ended and exploded and strands of coarse, greasy black hair in the disheveled sheets. Her violent new lover, who unlike Ruth did not sleep well. The table of photos is alone untouched — the photos are arrayed exactly as she had left them. Turds on the floor. Mementoes of a needy Adirondack Black bear.

She knows what she lacks and finds it in a second hand furniture store in Old Forge. Cracked wide down the middle — a free-standing full-length mirror.

Ruth Cohen has a plan.

◆ ◆ ◆

In the room reserved for those who will have direct contact with Saddam, the contents of their two bags are spread meticulously out on a long table, where a uniformed woman in surgical gloves is picking through the various items. She deposits Lucchesi's big-buckled cowboy belt in a metal box. Closes lid, cranks lever. The box hums and vibrates.

She says something. Mahmood translates: "Thank you very much, we have problem. The belt is declared innocent, the camera equipment hanging on the body of Ruth Cohen is also acceptable, but the backpack on your back is causing concern. In this room, we are investigating desire. Have you come to Iraq with a plan, she is saying?"

Ruth places her Leica in its strapped case, the tripod bag, and the large camera bag on the table — Lucchesi does likewise with the backpack.

The woman erupts.

Mahmood says, "She did not ask for Ruth Cohen to do this, because camera things are necessary for Saddam, we know this for 3 weeks. She is saying if the woman does another irregularity the gentleman who is totally expendable in Iraq must return to where he came from and the lady will stay to consummate friendship with Uday Hussein. You know Uday? She is saying camera things were properly investigated in Amman by Iraqi special agents, we know this, but the backpack formerly on your back must be understood completely. Dangerous people have infiltrated our country from your country, why should you be trusted, she is saying and I am agreeing, my dear friends?"

Lucchesi opens the backpack and reaches in, but she pushes his hand away and pulls out a copy of The Prostate Dialogues, inscribed "To Saddam Hussein, Fellow writer, may he be free from the concerns of this novel — struggle against chronic illness is fatal." She says, "Permitted" and takes out his toiletry case, unzips it and removes a small baggy of ear swabs, which she promptly deposits in a garbage can ("penetrating devices"), then 3 vials of medication, a tube of toothpaste, a homeopathic nasal spray decongestant, a jar labeled Tucks, a toothbrush, a second (and larger) baggy containing 80 vitamin tablets of 10 different kinds, 4 large bottles of Advil, a compact labeled Laura Mercier (because "I am a new, gender-flexible male"), an economy-sized tube labeled Personal Lubricant, 2 large paper clips, and another economy-sized tube, this one labeled Preparation H.

She deposits the toothbrush in the garbage can. Says something to Mahmood and makes a note. He translates: "She is writing to higher authority that you bring no toothbrush to Iraq."

Lucchesi says, "Very nice, bitch."

Ruth says, "Better make her happy, Lucky."

The woman speaks at length, Mahmood responds to her in Arabic. He translates: "Her cousin in Haifa Street sells lovely toothbrushes. Cheap. $12. I tell her you will buy 5 from her cousin in Haifa Street. That you will give her $60 (no dinars, please) to pass on to her cousin in advance of your visit to her cousin, to save time when you go to Haifa Street. Be happy, we are saving time. Give money to me, I will pass it to her in private. Thank you, Señor. The paper clips are No. She is suspicious of theoretical medications. Unsatisfactory explanation leads to special interrogation in special room with interesting interrogators."

Lucchesi responds, sadly, "This is for blood pressure, this for sleeping, this to help ease the urine."

Mahmood speaks to the woman, the woman replies with poignant eagerness. Mahmood translates: "She desires to know if pills for urination are useful for women because she is having such a problem you would not believe. I cannot survive much longer, she is saying."

"Does she have an enlarged prostate? Mine is the size of a basketball."

"Tell her to see a doctor — she has a bladder infection, the affliction of our gender."

"Under sanctions, only wealthy see doctors."

Ruth takes from her camera bag a vial of medication and says, "What every female traveler must not leave home without, my reserve of sulfa." She presents it to the woman, saying to Mahmood, "Tell her this is for the gender that lacks a prostate." The woman touches the shoulder of Ruth Cohen, the compassionate.

"Tucks. What is Tucks, Señor?"

"For hygiene in sensitive areas."

"Under sanctions, she is saying, her cousin's wife in Haifa Street is in need. Not for herself."

"Give her the jar and tell her not to be profligate at any given sitting."

"And Preparation H? Can this mystery be revealed?"

Lucchesi explains. Mahmood's pocket dictionary does not help. Lucchesi proceeds, as if he'd long prepared the moment, to make a series of sensational gestures.

The woman speaks plaintively.

"She is saying the H problem of her cousin's mother in Haifa Street is completely enormous."

"Tell her when the ointment is used up she should take a very hot bath daily for 20 minutes."

"She is insisting she herself lacks H problem. For her cousin's mother only."

Ruth says, "Dr. Lucchesi will apply it with his highly practiced finger. If she likes, as an alternative, he'll apply it deep with his dick. Tell her to request the alternative."

Mahmood forwards the message in toto. The woman blushes and laughs and says something. Mahmood says, "You are both extremely kind, you cause her to forget herself with such nonsense, welcome to Iraq and have a nice stay in Baghdad. We are watching you always. Especially the gentleman, who is totally expendable in Iraq. One more question and you may leave. Who is Laura Mercier?"

"An advanced formula concealer for the acne of my golden years."

"A consequence," Ruth adds, "of an excess of semen, backed up in his system. He can never get enough out, though he tries."

"She is saying that she would like to meet such a man, were he a Muslim, but under sanctions the supply of semen in Baghdad is very low."

Ruth says, "I like this bitch."

"She wishes to communicate that this bitch is a very big sense of humor, just like new American guests and youngest brother, Mahmood. Goodbye, may Allah bless you — and almost all of your countrymen. Mr. Lucchesi's drugs will be mailed to the United States when Mr. Lucchesi leaves Iraq."

Silence — the woman is smiling a fetching smile.

"You cannot confiscate my medications. That is a serious matter. Please."

"She is saying she is in complete agreement. There is time for comedy and time for seriousness. We have reached time of seriousness. So-called medications must be analyzed by Iraqi scientists. The buffoonery of Haifa Street is finished."

"This is outrageous. She cannot take my medications."

"She is saying if she wishes she can take you."

"Give me my medications back, I implore you."

"Mahmood is advising that you have no power."

The woman smiles, she winks.

Ruth says, "Forget it. In a week we'll be home. You can do without for a week. You'll live."

"She is saying you will leave Iraq when Saddam wishes. You will take pictures as Saddam wishes. You will live if Saddam wishes. You have very big toiletry case, congratulations. But in Iraq you are nothing. How do you like your brown-eyed bitch now, Mr. Lucchesi? She is saying."

On the way to the car, Mahmood asks about the camera. So small for such important work. Ruth explains that this Leica is splendid precisely because it's so light, so sleek and unencumbered, so sharp even without a tripod. Such qualities permit total freedom — maximize opportunities for spontaneity. She can move with the unposed subject. There is no moment with her Leica — Germany's smartest weapon of mass destruction, she says — that is disadvantageous for shooting Saddam — rapidly, repeatedly, and at will.

"Yes," Lucchesi says, "the Leica M6 is a thing of beauty, and a joy forever. Quite deadly."

Mahmood does not reply. Instead, he presents each of them with a special gift from Iraqi Airways — a watch displaying the happy face of Iraq's first mouseketeer: Saddam Hussein.

Thanksgiving morning, the gray light of overcast, and she's decided not to wear his watch cap, because neither did he on that hard bright day in January, long ago, when he sat there, huddled into himself, making notes on his long dead, his recessed father. Father of the averted gaze. Lucky sat exactly here.

She's standing bare footed and defiant in the iron cold, looking across the lake at the mountains, which have gone mostly brown, in this light virtually black, and utterly dumb.

Five feet from the water's edge, his metal folding chair (here, he sat, exactly here). Skims of ice, formed and thickened in the shallows, inch imperceptibly toward the deep and Ruth Cohen feels the wind knifing easily through his winter jacket, his heavy cords, his union suit, and she is reassured. She remembers: Ninth Lake is wrong, Ruth. Solitude and silence are wrong.

We were not meant to be monks. This is the message of Baghdad. I've been wrong about everything. This is what I'm learning in Baghdad — that life in a remote natural setting, however beautiful, is desiccation and death.

Come, January, my landscape of ice.

She sits, lost in his clothes — like Macbeth in Duncan's, as jays swoop and scream behind her. It faces the chair on uneven ground. It tilts right, the free-standing full-length mirror.

Come, January, and be my love.

From the manila envelope, the appropriate 8 by 10 — the one of him shot on that day, sitting here, where she now sits, where he took notes, bringing against the sub-freezing temperature of January a distant happy day in August, at the Black River camp, when he and his father played bocce with Tom Biamonte (then 10 years younger than himself at his moment of recollection) while his mother and Rose Biamonte prepared the Sunday meal — was it ravioli? It was, how delicious it was, and a salad of tomatoes and cucumbers fresh from Tom's garden (Tom is dead) and two lemon meringue pies. The beautiful Rose Biamonte is dead. As is his mother. Tom Biamonte — remember, Ruth? The story I never told about the man with the baseball bat. He entertained the kids on Mary Street, even the girls were fascinated by his dead-on imitations of the batting stances of the Yankees of the 1950s. Who me now? Yogi Bear! Thatsa who! Who me now? You no know? Why you no know?

Studies the photo and glances many times up at her tilted reflection, the off-centered woman in the mirror. She'll start with the feet. Checks the photo, checks the mirror. The feet are easy. Ruth, how tall is Saddam? She's arranging herself, sculpting her posture. The head tilt. Check photo, check mirror. The head is easy, I feel nothing. Does Saddam suffer from middle-aged spread? How many passes has he made? Do you return his smiles? Tell the truth.

From the jacket, a pen and small notebook. She'll put it all together. Pen poised over open notebook, head tilted slightly right, Lucky staring out at the lake and leaning, glazed, elbows tucked in, pigeon-toed, awaiting the seizure of time past, incarnated in a sensuous phrase, words (futilely pursued) that say, Cut me and I bleed time. She leans, she wants to lean in the direction of an elusive image, some flashing thing yet to be disclosed, just as he'd leaned that day in January, pen poised, toward a moment in August on the swift-running Black River, after the meal, when the women washed dishes and old Tom dozed (old Tom!) as he and his father sat close in the sun on a patch of struggling grass, with a transistor radio between them, listening through the static to the fading signal of a ballgame at Yankee Stadium — the feared Tigers of Detroit in town, with The Yankee Killer, Frank Lary, on the mound.

The cracked mirror splits her down the middle — in the outsized clothing her image is amorphous. Only the positions of feet and hands match what she sees in the photo. She feels nothing. I am a heap of borrowed clothes.

Joseph Stalin at any time and Omar Sharif in Dr. Zhivago, is what Saddam looks like, she'd responded. And he'd replied, Beauty and the Beast seamlessly blended in a single man — that's the secret of his charismatic power. A rare and irresistible combination. Did you resist? The restaurant with the dirt floor is on the broad and muddy Tigris of no refreshing breezes, in the district of neon, and middle aged strippers, who will say to me, Okay John Wayne want fuckey fuckey or lickey suck? Okay? The room will be full of perfumed and berobed Saudis in checkered head dress, who consult their palm pilots and then make arrangements for lickey suck only. And a bevy of slim and sleekly tailored Jordanian homosexuals on a night out at the heterosexual zoo, whose interest in lickey suck must be satisfied elsewhere. Daily I hit the wall of Arabic sound — incomprehensible and therefore consoling. A little like you, Ruth.

Cannot inhabit him. Can't bear this cold much longer, though I want to bear it a long, long time. Like a snowman.

As you work with Saddam, I stroll Baghdad and approach people to ask for directions and they hold up their arms as if to ward off demons and scurry away. Pedestrians and shopkeepers respond to my approaches by stating that their English is not exactly good, my dear man — without a hint of accent. These Iraqis I meet seem to think that a chat with me is the inside track to the electrodes and the dungeon. A woman shielded her baby — from what? My deadly gaze.

(These descriptions you bring me of Baghdadi life sound like writing. I am writing. Ruth! I'm writing again!)

She can bear no more and retreats to her cabin, trailed by his account of the climactic moment of that ballgame. Ruth is empty, except for a voice in the head that's saying, The dreaded Frank Lary had mastered the Yankees once again, allowing one run and two hits. The Tigers have scored three. In the bottom of the ninth, with two outs, Lary falters, or fakes faltering. He was faking. A walk and a hit batsman and now Mickey Mantle is striding to the plate, to do to Lary what he so richly deserves to have done to him, before a crowd of 67,000. The signal is weak, the static dense.

She sees it now at last, as she sculpts his time past out of the haze of that

August afternoon. The elusive image: The father saying — what? What should the father say? I'm sick and tired of this Lary. The son saying, Me too but Mickey never hits this guy. Lary is invincible. He's raising our expectations on purpose with the walk and hit batsman, he's toying with us, Daddy, so that he can crush our hearts when he strikes our mighty man out. Lary is cruel.

Young Lucchesi holding the radio up between them, the two heads leaning over the tiny speaker — this is how she wants it — the heads curling toward one another, almost touching, now touching! and the signal strengthening just because the heads touch, that's it, only because they touch the static disappears and Mantle gets a hold of it and drives it far and high into the bleachers. And the Yankees win. And their hearts were made glad. (He thought it was about baseball.) And their hearts were made one.

In her cabin, as she crawls into bed with his clothes still on, pulling up the covers, she saw what he'd never seen. What he'd never see. He who once said, We speak so often of my parents, so rarely of yours. I wonder why. Who are you, Ruth Cohen? Who are you, really?

She's well covered-up.

The sun dies on the Western horizon and darkness gathers fast — like a gloom condensed and motionless, brooding now over the ill-lit towers of the ancient place, the fabled city in the desert. Mahmood swings his government issue, late model Mercedes in the direction of Baghdad.

A big sky, like the sky of the American southwest. Palm trees. Bone-dry air. The chill of the desert night is already upon them.

Mahmood says, "No more semen jokes in Iraq, my friends. Okay? Bush number one makes cease-fire, but no cease-fire in the semen. Thank you, we are saying, for the low sperm count that is killing them in the wombs of their mothers. Thank you for the depleted uranium in our soil and water."

"It was a stupid joke," says Lucchesi from the back seat. He leans forward and puts his hand on Mahmood's shoulder — Mahmood's shoulder twitches.

"In Baghdad the birds are flying upside down. You must forgive my bitterness. Please. Babies born with holes where the eyes are supposed to be. How do you say? A blessing of disguise? In the zoo, they are feeding the lions carrots. I apologize for my bitterness."

An extended silence.

Ruth says, "So, this customs official is your sister. This is interesting to me."

"A way of speaking in Iraq. We have Iraqi blood together. Not family blood. This is of no interest."

Lucchesi says, "But she didn't say, according to your translation, my brother Mahmood. She said my youngest brother. Is that also a manner of speaking in Iraq?"

"Soon, maybe tomorrow, we will have massive sand storm. Very exciting. In sandstorms, we achieve privacy to think about who we are, and what is of interest, and what is not of interest, in our short time on this wounded earth, my friends."

Suddenly Baghdad — city of two skylines. One, perfectly horizontal, except for the punctuation of minarets and the nippled domes of mosques: this is the Islamic skyline of the picturesque, dirty old Baghdad of souks and inward-looking courtyard houses and the densely packed cellular structures of the traditional medina, a place of half-light and darkness, whose perpetually dampened and shaded streets are but narrow alleyways, where chickens and goats roam freely to forage in the strewn garbage: it is the quarter of Saddam's fierce anti-modern heart — the Saddam raised in a mud hut in Tikrit, who does not love the other skyline, the secular one of his creation: jagged with high-cut silhouettes of tissue boxes standing on end: new Baghdad, a perpetual construction zone of wide roads and roaring, undisciplined traffic, modern sanitation, shopping centers, German car dealerships, a subway system and above all (literally) the architectural repetitions that bespeak Saddam's penchant for the International Style. This is the city of Saddam's other heart, that loves godless modernity — the city where, nevertheless, among the double-decker buses, the ceaseless blare of horns, and the sea of taxis, on a divided highway you will see, at any given hour, men with full, jutting beards driving donkey carts heavy with produce, barefooted children, and black-veiled women.

"I have good news for you," Mahmood says, as he turns off the highway. "Change of plans. We do not go to Al-Rashid Hotel of journalists and spies. House of vipers. We are going to very rare house Saddam himself picks for you. House of the true Baghdad. Before Westernizing. Such a house is for you because serious artists do not love the inventions of the West, Saddam is believing, and Mahmood is agreeing."

In clogged traffic, at the edge of the old quarter, a boy of perhaps 6 or 7 approaches the halted Mercedes, presses his forlorn face (such big dark eyes) against the closed window on the front passenger side, and stares up at Ruth

Cohen. Stares and does not beg or speak. He's not holding in one hand for her observation some pathetic object, in hopes that this nice tourist will give him something, anything, for it. Instead, he's setting himself before her — he is himself the pathetic object. Ruth looks away. The car cannot move. She struggles to maintain a forward gaze. Does not want to look again. Does not want to remember the child in Havana, but her head turns anyway to the beautiful specter at the window. She tries to open the window, but Mahmood has locked all windows and doors. From the backseat Lucchesi says, "Give him this" and hands her a $5 bill. She asks Mahmood to release the lock. Mahmood says, bored, "If you want to do this, you can do this," and releases the lock. The boy steps back. She's thinking, How slight he is. She holds out the money. The boy does not take it. Ruth says, "Please." The boy's heart-breaking face has not changed its expression. He does not reach for the bill. Ruth says, "Please." A man rushes out of the crowd, snatches the bill, cuffs the boy hard, then drags him off by the collar, as the boy glances back, expression unchanged, and they are swallowed by the crowd.

Mahmood says, "Father and son business in the old quarter. The boy, Hassan, is famous."

The car cannot move.

Mahmood says, "Children are useful in Baghdad."

In her cold hands, the photo of Lucchesi with his thumbs in his ears, fingers in the flapping position: doing the donkey. She's recalling the night of his birthday dinner, when he'd demonstrated at some length his repertory of Neapolitan gestures, with special emphasis on the categories of scorn, derision, and stupidity. The lingua franca of Mary Street. Performed, he said, because civility demands it, only when the object of the gesture is not present. "You, Ruth, are a civilized person, and would not, therefore, perform them as I do now, when the object of my gestures is sitting directly across from me." How he'd laughed! She smiles faintly, briefly.

"These are the typical lineaments of the stupid ass, and therefore, in order to denote her, it is enough to imitate them. Ruth, watch! This is you:" Mouth opened, tip of the tongue on the lower lip, chin hanging, eyes half closed, and without any sign of vivacity or spirit. (At the cracked mirror, she makes the face. Holds it for a long time.) He laughed so hard he cried. He said, "Too bad

I couldn't drool — I'll have to work on it. Tomorrow, your assignment is to shoot me doing one of these, so that when I'm gone for good you'll have a reminder of who I really was, and what fun we used to have, when we were young and carefree." Said on the night of his 65th, she was 52.

The excited newscaster on Ruth's radio is saying that Saddam Hussein has been captured in a spider hole outside Tikrit — lice-ridden in full, wildman's beard. In his hand, not a revolver, or the requisite deadly tablet, but a copy of *The Old Man and the Sea,* while at maximum volume, on a battery-powered cassette player as Special Forces descend upon him, Sinatra singing "Strangers in the Night."

"One thumb in ear, palm and fingers oscillating slowly, is sufficient to indicate the ordinary donkey. Like this, up and down. When two hands are used, like this, like this, we express the superlative degree — *un stupido supremo.* That's us, Ruth, jackasses supreme. Because we live like hermits."

Crunch of dry twigs — under a wintry sun, Ruth the hermit walks the border of the blazing lake when a partridge flushes suddenly like whirling thunder beneath her feet and her heart is seized. Is this the end? She leans against a tree, looking waterward, transfixed by the glitter. Violence in the chest. The landscape tilts. Is this, then, the donkey's end? Alone in an idyllic setting, where no human sounds break the silence, too weak to cry out, were there any point in doing so. (Stupid ass.) "Nature," he'd said? "Nature is a natural disaster. We should go back to the house on Mary Street. That's where we belong." She sits. A loon passes before her, tilting, near the tilted shore, but here, at Ninth Lake, there are no loons. (He wanted loons to cry in the night, as he lay sleepless in his narrow bed.) She lies in the pine needles, in the fragrance of pine needles. Violence in the chest.

When you are normal, you do not feel it beating. That erratic jumping thing in your chest is the heart out of rhythm, when the blood flow constricts and you grow pale and cold — colder than you've ever been, though wrapped in three layers of winter clothing. Inhale the fragrance, Ruth, and breathe deeply, try to breathe deeply, though you cannot, and think the mantra that your doctor taught you: Inhale, calm, exhale, down. If you die, you may be found in the Spring thaw, as a pile of icy wet bones (how white they are!). Your body? Your body was an extended feast for raccoons, possums, crows, vultures, insects and worms. Your body was.

What had he said in Baghdad? He called himself the metaphysician of Mary Street. If you fall on Mary Street, you won't need to say your mantra more than once. Because Mary Street is where there is life. Mary Street is Utica's old quarter. Where deeds precede words and ideas. Where gestures are words. Where gestures and words cohabit, happily interdependent. Where, when there are no gestures, words are gestural — angular and lined with flesh. The voice on Mary Street is tissue, a single skin binding bodies in communication. Forget the worthless abstractions and embrace, and be embraced, by the sounds of voices. Better to be connected, he'd said in bed, in Baghdad. Listen for the grain of the voice, taste the skin of connection. I learn this about Mary Street in the cafes of the old quarter. She fights the sleep that would seal her up in final rest.

Leaning heavily on a crooked stick, she rises. Walks to the water's edge — to stare, be blinded and consumed by the fire on the lake. Violence in the chest. At the shore, looks back across the inlet to the two faded cabins. Death row, he'd called them on their second day in Baghdad, when she'd spent the late morning and afternoon with Saddam, at his Republican Palace. Picture-taking, an elegant lunch, picture-taking and conversation about picture-taking. The President is intrigued and quite eager, Ruth Cohen, to become acquainted with your philosophy of the camera. Be so kind as to enlighten him.

He wanted to talk only about the sound of Arabic voices. He spent the days in outdoor cafes, in the old quarter, thrilled, how fortunate he felt not to comprehend, he wanted to make that clear to her, how fortunate, not a single word, swept up and absorbed drinking mint tea, smoking the water pipe, shisha — he'd drifted, stoned on the mint tea and shisha, inhaling the peach-flavored tobacco, and the Arabic voices also inhaled. It was the thrill of something aurally manifest and stubborn, before the meaning of words, in no service of communication. What he heard were sounds unlike any he'd ever heard, delivering to his clueless American ear the pleasures of total opacity. Here, in Baghdad, in the absence of signification, a thing direct, the Arabic speaker's enfleshed voice, channeled to his astonished ear — he was wide open! — from deep in the speaker's cavities, his muscles, his membranes, his cartilages, telling a body without civil identity, in an impersonal voluptuousness of the tongue, the glottis, the teeth, the mucous membrane, the nose. A whole carnal stereophony — eroticism without desire and Lucchesi pulled to the other side, not afraid. Beautiful the amber liquid through the glass cup, the mint leaf afloat, his hands cuddling the hot glass cup, on a chilly day in Baghdad.

Sitting on a stone, the thing still jumping in her chest (inhale), Ruth puts her thumbs in her ears, fingers and palms flapping slowly (exhale), and emits a terrible sound, like the braying of a gut-shot jackass, and it's Father Michael's voice now in her head, saying Shit happens, Miss Cohen. And shit is unredeemable. (Sudden tranquility in the chest.) Father Michael says: A child's death is an abomination of God and an argument for atheism. You want theological explanation? Theology is not one of my tools. This child who died before your eyes. I'll not tell you that you bear no responsibility. You will suffer for that death for as long as you live. For as long as you breathe. Had you not gone to Cuba it wouldn't have happened. The logicians will argue that you are not the cause. But logic is not one of our tools, is it Miss Cohen? We find it empty. Why shut the door on such intimate events? Why even try? I can't relieve you. Wouldn't even if I could. Can't relieve myself . . . I spend my afternoons in hospitals, with the dying. We don't talk. We pray. They say, Hold my hand, Father. Then a beautiful nurse appears and I cannot pray, and I want to hold her hand. . . . Do you believe in God? A stupid question. God may not believe in us. . . . The child died, horribly, before your eyes. Were you a Christian I'd remind you that suffering is the significance of the Cross. Miss Cohen, your suffering is luminous because you suffer for another. Good. Very good! Most do not. Most suffer selfishly, in the dark. You're the latest Jew with a cross — a featured actor in the divine comedy. It may be one day you'll find cause in that to rejoice, though I doubt it. I wouldn't myself. "But was the child's suffering significant of anything but appalling darkness?" It's time, Ms. Cohen, to say goodnight.

(A dog might be the thing after all. An unstrokable dog.)

The exhausted foreign curiosities struggle through the al-Gailani souk, rolling suitcases behind them, as Mahmood parts the friendly crush — past the cafes of silent, heavy-lidded men they go; past the butcher shop, whose blood-slick carcasses hang in the open air (the fly-stickers of Old Baghdad); past the vendors of Saddam pencils, Saddam lighters; past the gleaming wares of the coppersmiths and the silversmiths, the aromatic stalls of roasting, marinated chickens and ravishing sweets, the hawkers of Saddam t-shirts, Saddam watches, Saddam posters; through the wash of Arabic and the arresting spectacle of Baghdadis in traditional dress; past the ancient reed weavers and now a startling boy, perhaps fifteen, a transported boy in a Chicago Bulls warm-up outfit, miming jump shot after jump shot. It is Dhafir al-Sayyid, who has no English, but when Lucchesi sings out "Michael Jordan!" he grins the mother of all grins, he forgets his game, forgets the roar of the crowd at Madison Square Garden, and joins the journey.

They turn off the souk into a deserted alley of doorways carved elaborately in geometric patterns — promises of a hidden world of elegance — but Ruth and Lucchesi are punished by a rigid blankness of walls, in a crooked corridor several donkeys wide, bisected with a gutter that runs a dark stream of viscous consistency, where feral cats feed by night. From the rooftops, accomplished fingers pick mournful melodies. The Americans have entered the labyrinth of Baghdad's suffering poor.

Mahmood rattles something rough-toned in Arabic. The boy runs off.

Lucchesi says, "Another of your beautiful and devious beggars?"

Mahmood ignores the question — "Here we are, be happy," and stops at a heavy wooden door, inlaid with ivory and mother-of-pearl, before which stand 2 impassive guards.

Down the long passageway — a dog leg left, so much the better to keep the eyes of the street from seeing within, and suddenly a gracious courtyard, a fine fountain at its center, with ficus in decorated pots arranged around the periphery. On a low teak table, near the fountain, catching spray, a golden bowl of dates and figs and a pitcher of pomegranate juice. With a gesture taking in the entire expanse of the three-storey colonnaded structure Mahmood says, "Your home for 5 days. Are you happy? I am very happy if you permit Mahmood to read your book for a day, because I have never read such a big American writer." Lucchesi grants the request, immediately, without correcting the characterization.

Then a whirlwind tour — because Mahmood has special business with his son, Dhafir al-Sayyid — through the daunting house of more than 2,000 square meters, of 115 rooms that vary in size from large domed reception halls on the first floor, with chandeliers in decorated brass, walls covered in ceramic tiles and splendid rugs and a dazzling filigree of joinery, to large and small rooms for living purposes, many of them giving on to the galleried second and third floors, overlooking the courtyard. No views to or from the street — "because Islamic architecture, my friends, is for protecting our secrets. Do you have secrets? Does the camel shit in the desert?" Eight full bathrooms in marble with domes of many-colored glass, molded and painted wooden walls and ceilings everywhere, doors inlaid with glazed metals everywhere, walls of windows of turned wood (floor to ceiling), colored marble mosaic floors, a number of underground tunnels, whose existence Mahmood does not bother to disclose, a maze of stairwells and hallways, arabesques and geometrics of fantastic interlacing complexity, foliate designs, floriated wood carvings, paneling perforated so as to spell out Koranic verses. "Where is the furniture?" "Saddam is despising clutter." "I feel lost and overwhelmed." "Me too." "You are not lost. You are in Baghdad." Lucchesi wants to know if the room with the mirrored ceiling might function as a bedroom and Mahmood replies, "Of course, Saddam is very sexual."

Mahmood explains the major functional division: diwankhana and haram, male and female spaces. "For privacy of the female, for respect of the female, this is also the message of Islam," then bids them goodnight, telling them that the 4 refrigerators are full, that the wife of one of the guards is at their disposal for cooking and laundry, "but not, please, for the monkey business of the mirrored ceiling."

Tomorrow, Saddam.

◆ ◆ ◆

In the examination room, alone and brooding, she awaits the entrance of Larry Shapiro, with whom she's had no appointments for a decade.

What occurred 3 days ago at 9th Lake had taught her, to her surprise, that she'd prefer to live a while longer — he might be alive. She prefers not to imagine evidence to the contrary, but she imagines it anyway: The gruesome, amateurish video, available on the world wide web. A letter: Dear Ms. Cohen, It is our solemn duty . . . in your grief.

She hasn't disrobed and donned the gown, though the nurse, proctologically inclined, insisted, Leave it open at the back. She's come only to make arrangements for a medical procedure, to request that the implantable defibrillator be soon implanted. You can't tie the gown in the back unless you're a contortion artist. . . . It always shows your ass. Is my ass falling? A minor surgery with all the risks spelled out in the brochure, puncture of the lungs, damage to blood vessels of the heart, infection, total failure of the device, massive coronary. Larry, who is not a surgeon, says that minor surgery is surgery performed on someone else. No need to disrobe and don the gown just to have a conversation whose point is, Let's do the defibrillator. It was a provisional decision — not the one to do the procedure, but the one to live.

In the past, before her arrival in Utica, it never embarrassed her when a male doctor examined her in her nakedness. With Larry, it was different. (Dear Ms. Cohen) She couldn't be sure, since nothing untoward was ever said, or even hinted. What a thought. Something in the way he responded when she visited — his difficulty in completing sentences, the sudden lapses, mid-sentence, as he reached for what turned out to be an ordinary word, or a medical term that he should have had well in hand. At times, a bit of a stutter. And his persistently averted gaze, that most of all, when he did examine her. In my nakedness. (We regret to inform you) Perhaps she was wrong about what those awkwardnesses signified, but she really didn't think so. When he gently slid the gown down off her shoulders to examine her breasts, gently, it wasn't fondling, it was an exam, wasn't it? When the gown fell back over her knees, mid-thigh, as she assumed the position in the stirrups, for the pelvic. . . . She thought he might be harboring — a man many years her junior, married with children, a kind man, a charming man, and a brilliant diagnostician with a mysterious power to make his patients feel healthy, even when they were not. (Results of DNA analysis . . . dental records confirm.) They left the clinic with a smile. They believed in him — he was the best medicine. With a profession full of Larry Shapiros the big pharmaceuticals would go broke, she once told him, and he'd blushed. Why did he blush? And what if he were harboring? Poor guy. Doctors have feelings too. How do they keep themselves from having that kind of feeling if they're having that kind of feeling? It's not as if they can say, I decide not to. You're seized. You're just seized. As I was, when I met Lucky. (It is my grievous duty, as Special Assistant to the Secretary of State) A person is just dragged along. What chance does anyone have against such a feeling? Larry had to look, touch me — what if he feels? — and put his finger. . . . Poor guy. She hopes that she's wrong, but she doesn't think so. Lucky's words, when we landed in Baghdad, were mischievously delivered: "A woman with a past and a man, at 71, looking for a dramatic future." (I think Lucky's dead.)

My tits are falling. The sky is falling. This varicose vein. My hearing is going. . . . Whatever fantasies he feeds his heart on, oh the sight of me now — it's been a long time — will cure the good doctor for good, if you can be cured of that. But what if he doesn't want curing? Lucky never said a word. Reacted as if I'd never changed. As if he and I were 25. Always made me feel 25, the way he went at me, but now that he's gone I notice my body — falling everywhere. (Word out of Iraq: today the remains of American writer Thomas Lucchesi.)

Larry enters not in standard white coat but in a beautifully cut blue blazer, a smashing sports shirt, stylish tan slacks, and shoes shined to a hard, glossy finish. Why isn't he wearing his white coat? He's prepared, all turned out (for me?) but inside the spiffy ensemble it's still the same old Larry whose behavior tells her what she thinks she'd rather not know.

"Ruth, it's so good to . . . I mean . . . I'm sorry for your loss."

"He may not be lost in that sense. We can't be sure. . . . How are you and the family, Larry?"

"Good. Good. Kerry's a junior at Kennedy, I can't believe it, and Kathleen turned two in August. The terrible twos. Good to see you, Ruth."

"Good to see you too."

An uncomfortable pause.

"And your wife?"

"Megan. Good. Megan's good. We're all good. How can I help you?" Fiddling with his ballpoint pen and clip board.

And if she knew, for sure, that Lucky were dead? Give the good doctor what he wants? Why not? What's the difference? Matters more to them than to us. They think too much of it, about it. Men. Lucky. Larry. Once he sees what he's getting, gotten, if he can actually go through with it, not with his fingers this time in me but with his, in this old lady, the good doctor will be cured for good. Drain off his every drop of fantasy and then when he goes home without his fantasy he can be there full time in his mind, then he'll become real at last, at home, and when he makes love to Megan it will be Megan, the actuality of her flesh and tongue and not some ghostly presence, ghastly me that he's. . . . But if he's not cured by my deteriorating body? I'm leaving my wife and kids because I. . . . What a horror. No, I wouldn't do it. Why would I want to again if Lucky? From the grave, if that's where he is, he'd haunt me. See, I told you you would betray me when I'm dead. I want my husband back. Where is he?

"It's settled, then, good," he's saying, "I'll arrange everything at St. Elizabeth's. It's an outpatient thing, 3-4 hours tops, a follow up 3 days later, then another one in about 10 days, and that's pretty much it. I'm glad you've made this decision, Ruth. Because you're young and you're still —"

"No I'm not, but thank you anyway. Speaking of St. Elizabeth's, I visited Charley DiStefano in the nursing home across the street."

"Did he know who you were?"

"His eyes grew wide when I approached him. He was slumped in his wheelchair. He didn't talk. I said, Nice to see you again, Uncle Charley, and his eyes grew even wider."

"He hasn't walked, rarely speaks, since the stroke. I get reports from my colleague, Corinne DiMarco. She'd make a good doctor for you if you'd like to make a change, I wouldn't take it personally."

(I was wrong. Or he's gotten over it. Or he's testing the water. Or he wants to get over it. Am I disappointed? Why should I be?)

"He spoke to me, Larry. Ten or fifteen minutes after I said Nice to see you again, Uncle Charley, he lifted his head. I hardly recognized him. He said, Nice to see you too, dear. I said, Are you in pain? He replied, It doesn't tickle. His voice was almost familiar: a hint of immortality. He looked terrible. Skin and bones."

"How long did you stay?"

"About an hour and a half. Just before I left he said, I can't be expected. I touched his hand and he said again, I can't be expected. I said, We can't be expected. Nobody can. When I left I noticed an odor."

"He probably hasn't had control of his bodily functions since the stroke. What? Ten years ago? They change their diapers several times daily. It's an excellent facility."

"Lucky feared that."

"Who?"

"My husband. Feared that might happen to him at the end. Said, if it did, I should shoot him. He may never have to deal with that fear. A consolation, I suppose. I think they murdered him. Of course, if he's really gone he's nothing and the consolation, such as it is, is mine."

"I hope he comes back to you soon."

"I think they murdered my husband. . . ."

"Ruth, I want to ask you something. I may be out of line. If I am, please forgive me."

(Here we go.)

"Yes?"

"I was . . . I mean I am fond of Thomas, but . . . and think about him often. . . . I wonder if you'd mind telling me what he was like in Baghdad. Was he happy? I need a happy image of him in Baghdad. This is childish and totally unprofessional, but I feel that I'm more than a physician to you and Thomas. I need a happy image. Do you have one?"

"Even if I have to lie?"

"Yes."

"I'd like to tell somebody, and who do I know aside from you? I don't mean that the way it sounds. You mean a great deal to the both of us."

"Thank you for saying so. You mean a great deal to me too. The both of you, I mean."

"Larry, I don't have to tell you a benign lie. He was happy. He really was. He was absorbing the life of a culture utterly foreign to our experience. He would have said it was absorbing him, and that's why he'd come back at dinner time like a large child who's finally gotten what he wants. How's that for the happy image you requested?"

"Perfect."

"It's true. And he was writing again, he told me."

"About Baghdad."

"About Utica. East Utica. Mary Street. He said that Baghdad gave him the desire to write about life rooted in a place. Organic culture is how he put it. He was finally going to write his Utica novel, and do it right. Organic fiction. He'd finally cast aside the old lacerating need to write a political book worthy of Cuban Stories. He believed Baghdad would make him a political artist. But Baghdad had the opposite effect. He thought we should move back to Mary Street. He was very happy."

"He was fulfilled."

"Yes."

"A lucky man. Who gets to be fulfilled?"

"Fulfillment with a bad ending."

"And you came home to all that disturbing publicity. CNN and the *Times*. They came here trying to find you. The tabloids. Return of The Scarlet Photographer. We sent them all to Old Forge. How did you manage to avoid the paraparazzi?"

"I greeted them all with my shotgun."

"Father Michael would have been proud of you. You said no to the devil."

"Give my best to your wife."

"I shall."

"Give her yours, too, doctor."

"As often as I can, Ruth."

◆ ◆ ◆

She had anticipated the excesses of marble and gold at the Republican Palace on the western edge of the Tigris, but not the simplicity of this underlit room into which she is ushered, with its great windows open to the river, bone white walls adorned with no pictures, no rugs, nothing at all; a floor of rough-textured concrete, painted black; a long table of inexpensive wood (parson's style, she thinks, noting with an inner smile the cultural irony of the analogy), finished in clear lacquer — barren except for a pitcher of ice water and 3 glasses; and a ceiling of gracious height, also in black.

He's seated behind the table, at the center, his broad back to the brown-rushing river. The translator, Habib Aziz, is seated at the far end. They rise in unison. Habib is a short, thin man, forgettable in traditional robe, headdress, and sandals, a recent graduate of Oxford, M. Phil., whereas (the contrast has been arranged) the Leader cuts a blazing figure — tall and powerfully built, impeccably groomed and subtly cologned in a silk pin stripe suit, custom tailored in London, with a maroon handkerchief of white striping fluffed a little outrageously in his breast pocket: a touch of the old reprobate, the secret decadent, in this ascetic space of his design. Such luxuriant wavy hair — very good looking by any standard, Ruth thinks. An opinion she'll not pass on to her husband, and one she wishes she hadn't had.

The translator stands at the table as Saddam ("the one who confronts") comes forward to greet her. She puts out her hand and he takes it in both of his, with a slight bow of the head, speaking in Arabic with lyrical intonation. The translator says, "The President wishes you to know that your pleasure is his. That you have only to speak your pleasure, Ruth Cohen, and it shall be granted."

She loads her camera, saying, "This" — holding up the camera — "is my pleasure." Habib translates for Saddam, Saddam replies, and Habib translates for Ruth: "The President admires the commitment of a serious artist. He is himself a writer who has published 3 novels." Saddam taps the table with his pen and speaks. Habib translates: "Forgive me, 3 fictions in the classic mode of romance. Not novels. As an Oxford graduate I should know this generic distinction. It is conceivable that I am not my father's son, the President is saying."

Saddam comports himself with this foreign guest as he has comported himself with no other. When he addresses her, he does not look at the translator, as is his wont, or at the pen turning constantly in his hands. He looks at her directly, never averting his gaze, and speaks with rare animation, with no trace of his typically phlegmatic, virtually thick-tongued manner — as if they shared the language, and so much else. She will find him charming and warm and feel the frightening urge to trust him. How difficult he makes it to credit the reports of a butcher who sanctions torture and mass killing, who himself had done murder when young, and when not so young — without emotion, they said, no rage, in ice cold will.

She will try to keep herself from thinking that he is easy to like, but she will fail. She will remember (to little avail) that persons of fame and power, in person, obliterate all the horrific reports, by sheer shattering presence. That they are, like erotic fantasies, virtually beyond resistance.

An aide appears with a third chair. Saddam gestures for her to sit. The camera is slung sexily around her neck. She places her tripod bag on the floor next to the chair — on the chair itself her large camera bag bearing extra batteries, 2 back up camera bodies, a portrait lens, a flash unit, 20 rolls of 36 exposures each, and the inscribed copy of The Prostate Dialogues, returned by Mahmood that morning. She'll have no use for the tripod, the flash unit or the portrait lens. This will be intimate and candid work, of hundreds of shots, mostly of the head and upper torso.

She says, "Thank you. I have come to work, not to sit and converse." Saddam smiles; Saddam likes Ruth.

He speaks in a tone that says, "Of course, we agree, how could we not?" Habib translates: "The President asserts that in good company we may both work and converse. Are you sympathetic?" Before she can reply Saddam speaks harshly to Habib, who corrects himself: "The President does not assert, he suggests, that in good company we may work and converse hand in hand. Are you sympathetic?"

She realizes that Saddam understands English perfectly — and likely speaks it fluently. Nevertheless, she'll not trim her words. She replies, "Inform Mr. Hussein that my camera has a built in light meter which requires that I approach him frequently. To place it within a few inches of his moustache."

Saddam is pleased. Unlike Ruth Cohen, the Leica M6 will prove to be adequate to the challenges of its subject.

Habib says, "The President wishes to convey that he has no fear. The President is asking, Do you? He requests that I tell you that in the village in which he was raised, conversing is considered equivalent to playing. To have conversation with good company is to have the most intimate of pleasures. And in such pleasure, the poor of his village are as blessed as the wealthy of Baghdad. Feel free, he says, to approach frequently."

As she approaches, Saddam turns in his chair and gestures toward the windows and speaks softly and briefly. "The President says that the river is a strong brown god." Saddam, again briefly. "The river is untamed and intractable." Saddam nodding now, speaking at greater length. "The brown god is forgotten, unpropitiated and dishonored by the dwellers of this great city, but not by the people of his village, whom it destroys in its implacable rages." Saddam turns back in his chair to Ruth, speaking as she shoots him close, hovering over the brooding philosopher. "As a youth I swam often in the river, and now the river is inside me. I do not know much about the brown god, I do not know what it means, only that its rhythm pulses in my blood and that I would write sentences like the waves on the river, because then, truly, I would be a writer of force."

(Lucchesi, the prey, strolling aimlessly in the old quarter, followed at a discreet distance by Dhafir al-Sayyid, whose father, Mahmood, had lectured him sternly the night before on his repeated acts of truancy. They reach a crowded square, where the boy makes a wide half-circle, then turns and bears directly down on Lucchesi, who does not notice. When he's within 5 feet, Dhafir shouts Michael Jordan! Lucchesi, without Arabic, grateful for a companion, bows a deep theatrical bow and gestures for the truant-without-English to join him.)

Saddam unbuttons his jacket, sits back and spreads his knees, revealing crotch and belt buckle, with an inscription in Arabic. Because when you fight the Great Satan you must fight satanically. Consequently, he had instructed Habib to do research on American poses, and Habib had shown him Banana Republic advertisements in *The New York Times Magazine*.

Ruth snaps numerous full body shots, as she slowly circles the subject. As if reading her mind, Habib says, "The inscription signifies, This is Saddam's belt." Saddam says something and laughs. Habib says, "He wishes to add what is not on the belt, just for you, a very special guest: Abandon all hope, ye who venture below."

She goes to the camera bag to withdraw Lucchesi's novel. Saddam follows. She gives him the book. He holds it, front jacket facing her, as she snaps shot after shot. (One year later, the photo will adorn the front jacket cover of the

Knopf reprint.) He asks Habib to translate Lucchesi's inscription ("Struggle against chronic illness is fatal"). Saddam speaks with sudden gravity. Habib translates: "Iraq is America's chronic illness and Little Bush struggles fatally, like Big Bush, with the failure of his leadership."

(They walk in silence toward a park and a soccer field by the river, Lucchesi in Dhafir's tow, thinking, This is what it must be like to be the father of a son, and Dhafir pointing at that very moment to Lucchesi, saying, "Abu Dhafir" (father of Dhafir), which Lucchesi does not, of course, understand. Lucchesi thinking, This is what it must be like to be the father of a teenage son. You don't understand one another. You don't speak the same language. And yet you wish to be close to one another, though you don't know how to communicate such a thought — it is too embarrassing. So you walk together in intimate and painful silence. And many years later, when you are separated by geographical or emotional distance, or both, likely both, or by the death of your son, or your father, you remember that day of the walk to the park by the river, when you could not say to him the things that you wanted to say, and never in your life said.)

For Habib's second assignment in the satanic lore of American poses, Saddam had directed him to acquire photo books of JFK, so that Saddam could enact for The New Yorker certain Oval Office pictures of Kennedy, long burned into American memory. The one where he's standing back to camera at the front of the desk, leaning stiff-armed on the desk, head tilted down, hunched over, as if reading. Directly behind the desk, a large window, so that, backlit, JFK is a darkened figure of concentration, a great man focused on the work of his people, though I truly do not believe, Saddam thought, that he was reading, or even much thinking. I believe that in this picture Kennedy was doing what I so often do. Mourning his loneliness. Or the profile shot at the window in silhouette, in the most familiar of his postures: hand in jacket pocket, elbow jutted out. What was he thinking? Nothing. He was posing in America. Kennedy was less than his pictures. That was why they killed him. We have the picture. The person is totally disappointing. Kill him, oblige him with death, because he does not wish to be less than his picture. In my village, we care not for pictures. In a mosque, no images. I have permitted many of myself, like an infidel, who with these pictures of himself for America wishes to subvert the infidels with images that say, Behold the man, Saddam Hussein! A person very like you. Am I less than my picture? No doubt.

So many conspiracies, so few to trust. Perhaps they will kill me too. I have killed so many who wish with complete malignancy to kill me, but I have not yet killed everyone who wishes to kill me. After all, one cannot kill everyone, not even in Iraq — so broods Saddam, as Ruth, who knew the Kennedy pictures well, shoots him many times as JFK.

Let me be fortunate with this woman as Kennedy, they say, was fortunate with her — he, who like me, was fortunate with so many. She is not young, but is thrilling still and it would be thrilling to be with her, God willing, who was with the enormous American myth.

Like Kennedy, I will be destroyed. The great Hemingway teaches that a true man will always be destroyed, but never defeated. I, Saddam Hussein, was not born for defeat, God willing.

(No prostate medication for 2 days and he's feeling the effects: slow, painful, and meager urination every 30 minutes, and now, on the streets of Baghdad with this boy, what can he do? The cafes offer no rest rooms. The restaurants are closed and no public facilities in sight. How can he indicate his problem to the boy without making in gesture what could only be taken as an untoward suggestion? Twice he finds an alley, gestures for the boy to wait, follows it behind a building and relieves himself, like a dog, against a garbage bin in the first instance and a moribund date palm in the second. When they reach the park, he needs to once again and disappears into a vast thicket of bamboo.

Thanks to his cunning decision at breakfast to take no fluids, with the exception of a single large glass of juice, and thanks to the rigors of a long brisk walk on which he'd worked up a splendid sweat, he finds himself, as he emerges from the thicket, at last symptomless, truly relieved, and a little light-headed. He's suffering from first stage dehydration, though he doesn't yet know it, as he and the boy meet at the soccer field 2 other truants of Dhafir's acquaintance and choose sides: it's Lucchesi and the 2 new boys versus Dhafir, the Pelé of Baghdad, as he's known at school. Like his team, Lucchesi will soon find himself in serious trouble.)

An aide in chef's hat and apron wheels in a serving cart. He's about to set places for lunch when Saddam says something to him, causing the aide to turn and leave, but when he reaches the door Saddam again speaks, and the aide returns, removes his hat and apron and gives them to Saddam, who promptly dons hat and apron, wheels the cart to the table, sets the places, picks up the soup ladle and has an idea. Habib tells Ruth, "He wishes for you to take his picture." Ruth tries, but fails to hide her amusement. Saddam has caused her to smile and Saddam is happy. She snaps Chef Hussein's photo many times. One of these becomes the opener in The New Yorker photo essay.

He begins to serve. As he ladles the soup into Ruth's bowl he has another idea, which he communicates to Habib, who says, "The President would be greatly honored if you would make it possible for me to take your picture with him, as he serves you." She says, "Brilliant," and instructs Habib, who snaps several photos of the grinning Chef and his guest. When he's finished serving the lentil soup, the lamb on a bed of dill rice, the sides of yogurt and mixed pickles, he sits to partake with his guest, having removed the apron but not the hat — eager to discuss Ruth's philosophy of photography, while softly in the background, piped through speakers artfully hidden in the four walls — Sinatra, "It Had to be You." Habib says, "Saddam loves Frank Sinatra." Saddam replies and Habib says, "But not Bing Crosby."

The time is propitious, as he guesses. Intimacy with this woman is his destiny. In English, he dismisses Habib. She does not give him the satisfaction of a surprised reaction.

"What I intend," she says, trying but failing to avert her gaze, "as a photographer, never comes out as I intend it."

"What I intend," he toasts her, "always comes out as I intend it."

"I stand in front of something, instead of arranging it. I arrange myself."

"I have always found it a pleasure to arrange others."

"Geometry is the supreme pleasure, the corroboration of absolute structure. I desire that geometric values be the end of my art, but I have failed to achieve my end."

"You do not desire to represent the stories of individuals in your art?"

"I do not desire to represent anything."

"Then we agree completely. It is torture to represent individuals, and I prefer not to be tortured. Better to give than to receive."

"The stories of individuals cause pain."

"To you?"

"Yes."

"Better to give than to receive."

She's not touched her food.

"I would make a photograph as an altogether new object, complete and self-contained, whose basic condition is order, inside the independent world of the photograph."

"Unlike," Saddam replies, with sudden intensity, mouth full, spitting particles, "the actual world of events and actions, whose permanent condition is change and disorder and ugliness."

"Yes."

"We are in complete sympathy, Ruth Cohen."

"But I have failed to achieve my artistic desire."

"I do not fail," cutting into his lamb.

"In your fiction?"

"Fiction is my minor art."

"What is your major art?"

"I think of myself as the artist-President, who sculpts his raw material, the Iraqi people, into the condition of absolute structure, free of the disorders of change. Ruth Cohen, how do you like my hat? Do I amuse you? Do you think that I am a clown?"

Sinatra: "I've Got You Under My Skin."

Ruth thinks, This is terrible. This is truly terrible. I feel no fear. No revulsion. None whatsoever, in the presence of this monster.

(He's pale, faint and cold. He vomits. Frightened, the 2 truants they'd met at the field run off. Lucchesi says to Dhafir, "Did the Yankees win?" Dhafir races to a nearby vendor, who gives him (free of charge) 2 large bottles of water. When Dhafir returns, he finds a man in a black leather jacket, kneeling at Lucchesi's side. It is his father, who'd come to the park when he learned at Dhafir's school that his son was absent again. Dhafir attempts to remove Lucchesi's backpack but Mahmood, boiling in irritation over his son's truancy, takes it roughly from him, saying there's no chance in hell that Dhafir will receive an actual basketball for his birthday. Mahmood covers Lucchesi with his jacket and Dhafir administers small doses of water (32 ounces) for 45 minutes, at the end of which Lucchesi has recovered his color, his lucidity, and his need to pee. Dhafir and Mahmood, arms around him, assist him to his feet and to the edge of the thicket, where Mahmood orders his son to stay put for no reason other than a repeatedly defied father's need to assert the fantasy of his authority. They enter the thicket. When they come out, Lucchesi is smiling, saying, "The pause that refreshes." Mahmood gives Dhafir money to purchase lunch, but the vendor refuses payment, reminding the boy of the beautiful practice of Arab hospitality, particularly when a foreigner is in need, even if the foreigner is an American. Directly across the river, some 500 yards away — at the Republican Palace, where Ruth and Saddam discuss the virtues of nonrepresentational art and politics — a surveillance team, responsible for security at the park along the Tigris, prepares a report, for Saddam's eyes only, on the behavior of Special Agent Mahmood al-Sayyid and the husband of the American photographer.)

She stands on the table, at the end of a long afternoon. He sits with his back to her, looking directly at the ceiling. She shoots down on his face: Saddam inverted. He leans forward in his chair, right elbow propped on knee, hand up, fingers spread wide: staring at his palm as she shoots lying on the floor. Then, within a foot of Saddam — his eyes, his glittering eyes. Finally, with 3 exposures left in the last roll, a use for the flash unit: classic mug shots in harsh light.

He rises and approaches with a bold stare. She says, "As a photographer I learned that nothing you plan will ever come to life."

"And that is precisely why I always plan with the utmost care. My fair lady, stay the evening and we shall dine and discuss the sad failure of Godfather 3."

"Goodbye, Mr. President — I loved that movie."

She's naked, white-bodied, a ghost pulling over ice and snow the cracked, free-standing mirror, when she slips and falls hard, clinging to the mirror as it comes shattering down upon her in a thousand shards. (Good. Smash all cameras too.) Blood on the snow. (Good.)

Quick! Arise and dance naked for the missing man. Resurrect him with salacious gyrations. For once, make yourself a clown — as he had on so many occasions made himself a clown for you, to retrieve you from your brooding remoteness.

Look! How he leaps in desire! (Whose desire?) Here he comes, all the way back on this bitter day — past all difficulty leaping, convulsed in laughter he leaps past death itself. (Is my husband dead?)

When will you dance?

She bleeds from several small cuts on her hands and one on her inner thigh. (Where he lingered.) Scoops snow in both hands and presses it against her breasts. (Where he sucked. But no babes sucked.) Rises and retreats to the cabin, to put on his robe, tend to her wounds, stoke the dying fire. Or maybe not. (Quick! Go out and finish the job. Your first work of performance art: The Abominable Snow Woman.)

I wonder if there's any hot chocolate? (He would have said.) Because these, Ruth, are the halcyon days of hot chocolate and hot sex. Maybe someone will make me a cup of hot chocolate, not because I'm incapable of doing it for myself, but because it tastes so much better when you do it for me. Piping hot, on this terrible day. Put a little whipped cream on top and I'll return the favor, I'll whip up concupiscent curds, just for you. I feel today as if in my great good luck I'd married a nurse. Or a girl just like the girl who married dear old dad. (Dead. Unnursed.)

Shuffling about the cabin in his slippers, sipping hot chocolate. (This is his blood.) Pauses, long, opposite the place on the wall where the big fork he'd thrown that time had struck and gouged. Touches the gouged place. (I do this in memory of you.)

A bath, as hot as she can bear it, lowering herself weeping into the tub, remembering again, how many times? . . . Lies back in the steaming bath, wanting to smoke again, wanting to drink too much, wanting to sleep all day and all night in the hot bath of her last pleasure, reviewing like the phrase of a song in her mind that repeats relentlessly, it drives her to the edge, this fantasy of heroic Ruth, the fantasy of somehow — in the chaos of the American occupation, somehow getting into Iraq, overland from Jordan, stowed away in a truck hauling produce for Baghdad and somehow. . . . No medications. No hot chocolate. 71 years old. With just a pen and in his back pocket — her final sight of him — as he walked away and turned to say his last words — he would have called it his exit line — patting the notepad in his back pocket, "To catch the last forced trickle of my creative energy. As a man pees, so does he write." No goodbye because why would he? Had she smiled? Did he? She can't remember. Did she say hurry back? Ruth, he would have said, if he knew — it would have been just like him to have said it, "This is a culture for which I can well imagine losing my head."

The mind is its own place — how he loved to quote the classic poets, the dark ones, especially those in their darkest moments. They made him happy. Try laughing, he said. Try the black-hearted poets for comedy. Myself am hell. You too, Ruth, laughing.

Turns on the hot water spigot, slides down deeper in the tub, submerged to the chin — my severed head afloat. The terror of the dark, he said joyfully at breakfast. He'd been awake since 4. Sleep badly with me and await the vanquishment of the dark, when the voice at dawn calls to prayer. Come, come, prayer is better than sleep! Pray with me! There is no God but Allah and Mohammed is his prophet. Surrender, surrender! Islam is surrender!

What have we surrendered, Ruth? What have we given in our separate cabins, where the spider weaves our last will and testament? Do we know any of God's 99 names?

Come, come to the mosque — sings the voice from the minaret — all who hear come and praise God. A tower beside a mosque. For vocal projection. In honor of the voice. (He was so eager, a schoolboy bringing home his lessons.) The al-Gailani mosque, he said, and a school, a public bath, a public fountain, a souk. In all these places they gather. With whom have we gathered? In the vicinity of the voice, whose aural reach defines the neighborhood, they gather. Nearness is all. What voice have we heard at Ninth Lake? (Nearer, my God, to nobody.) The voice in long arching and aching lines — the breath control! The fluidity! A river of sound traversing the registers of lamentation and ecstasy, I cannot tell the difference, winding down the streets and alleys — saturating the public square, curling about the houses and cafes, commandeering the souk, lingering over the rooftops, waking the goats and turkeys, soothing the dogs who will not howl, rubbing its sinuous phrases against the window panes, licking its tones into the corners of resistant night, and night falters, as the voice drinks the dark down to the dregs.

He'd asked Mahmood, What is the precise moment of dawn? How is it determined? And Mahmood told him that the singer in the tower holds up before him in the pitch of night a single black thread — its visibility is dawn, and the launch of his voice.

He wanted to test Mahmood's story. The next day at 4 A.M. Could I provide a thread? Would I listen with him? Be swept up with him? I don't like to be alone, Ruth.

She'd never seen him like that. The floating head smiles a little, remembering how beside himself he'd been that morning. He'd put himself aside. He'd surrendered.

There is a voice, Mahmood had told him, from the other side of the Tigris. Unamplified. Some say it is true. Winding across wide water. Nonsense, others are saying. Allah akbar! You could hear it at dawn, even from this side of the

Tigris, if you were devout. So many of us are not. I am not. If you had truly vanished into God. So many of us desire the things of the West. I do not hear the voice. Are you wishing to hear as a devout Muslim? Are you needing to disappear? I am thinking that Ruth Cohen desires it more. (Put ourselves aside. What Lucky wanted for us. Together to relinquish the selves of our isolation.)

She takes a deep breath and goes under, but cannot stay under long enough.

Comes up gasping, remembering the night in Baghdad, when he said, We've made love in the harem. We're horny infidels. Tonight we violate the oldest unwritten law of this culture — the code of social restraint that Saddam violated by building this 3 storey extravaganza in the midst of 2 storey houses, which used to be the limit when Baghdad was entirely an old quarter, when they respected the privacy of the family without exception. (Professor Lucchesi.) Before the exception of Saddam, whose philosophy is, Your privacy is my business, because in your privacy you hatch plans for my death. Better you than me. Did he make a move on you, Ruth? (You'll never tell the truth, or I'll never believe your response, so don't bother answering.) In the long hot summer these people take to the roofs in the evening. On a mild night like tonight they'll be out there. The high roof walls make it impossible for one family to spy on another. Thanks to Saddam we can survey old Baghdadi life in its hidden authenticity. We'll see, but not be seen. And when we've sated ourselves with feasts of the eye, we'll do something on the roof, which is why I'm bringing these 3 blankets. To cushion our ancient bones. One more for the road. Because we're not quite sated.

As she gazed, she lost herself, dissolved into the objects and scenes of her contemplation — she was filled to the brim with the roof life all around them: A man writing by candle light. A woman watching television. A boy and a girl kicking a soccer ball, practicing headers. The ball flying over the parapet. Meat on a grill over an open fire. Flamboyantly colored undergarments, fluttering on a clothes line hung between the chicken coop and the pigeon coop. A tethered goat. A teenage girl gazing at the moon — a boy gazing at the girl. An old woman ironing. Six people seated around a low table, a few inches off the floor, eating. Men at board games. A Coke sign, circa 1955. A flower garden. An herb garden. In the corners, the jumbled debris piles — pieces of pipe, broken ceramic tiles, a door, scrap lumber, scrap sheet metal, broken glass. In the far distance, many open fires. Many satellite dishes.

Pathetic what I retain: a dead list, a mechanical enumeration of objects, but the life swirling on those roofs, swirling even in the debris piles and the outright garbage, where has it gone? The life that swirled me that night. Where is it? Gestures, odors, voices. The gaiety and the solemnity. Cannot call it up, has left no residue.

Who am I? A mind of winter. I've been cold a long time. No difference now between the memories of that night and those of the reception hall at Heathrow, on the return trip. All stale and inert — like a series of photographs. Chocolate Box, Sunglass Hut, Chanel, Burberry, Bureau de Change, Rolex, 24 Hour Cash, 24 Hour Money.

In the distance we could see the al-Gailani Mosque, named for a legendary mystic. There, once a week, the dervishes whirl out to God. In ecstasy, they put themselves aside.

She opens the cabin door and steps naked into the mean wind, the slanting snow storm, and begins to whirl.

8 ◆ Two Codas

FROM THE BOOK OF RUTH (2005)

"THE GEOLOGY OF LOVE"

About a year ago, we were flattened on an August afternoon at 9th Lake by record levels of heat and humidity. He proposed that we seek relief in the homeopathic method (his actual words). Afterwards, he rolled over and picked up the 983 page tome on my bedside table, Geology of the Adirondacks. To that point, he had shown no interest in my new reading. He shook his head and said, I don't know Ruth, I don't know. Then, naked, he stood and walked around to my side of the bed and said, What has this (holding up the book in one hand) to do with this (with the other hand touching himself). This (touching himself) is the thing itself. This (penis still in hand) is love. We laughed. What has this (waving the book) to do with this (waving his penis), or this — and he dives down quickly and brushes his tongue across my vagina, then crawls over me back to his side of the bed, saying as he crawls, There is, there can be, no geology of love.

Generally, I'm not up to the task of riding his metaphors, but this time I was primed. I say, It isn't true, then proceed to give him my short course on plate tectonics — how continents, separated by oceans, like lost lovers longing for one another, seek each other out. A journey of several hundred million years. The ocean between them closes. The ocean crust, the ocean's very floor, rammed persistently from behind, dives deep down beneath the awaiting continent, thanks to the force of the approaching lover, the propelling and propelled continent. He asks, Continents and ocean floors are in constant motion? Yes, I reply, continents and ocean floors are crustal plates, like large patches of scum, afloat on boiling water, and driven by thermal plumes from below. As the ocean crust dives deep and hard beneath, it produces unimaginable heat and pressure. Volcanoes are thrown up, eager to explode their lava all down the flanks of themselves, flooding the basin below.

What about the approaching continent, the aroused lover, he wants to know? Does it ever make actual contact with the awaiting continent, the one that needs to receive? Does it ever, I say. And the moment of continental collision produces orogeny. (Erogeny, he says?) Crust at the continental margins is crushed and deformed, slabs of the plates override each other, and the crushed crust is thrown up high and folded. This is orogeny, a mountain-building event which occurs when continents come together. Mountains higher than the Himalayas, born hard. This moment, Lucky, this event, a mere punctuation mark in geological time — think of these crazy words, event and moment, how crazy they are inside the idea of geological time. Plates moving at the rate of 2 millimeters a year. Think of the extended foreplay. Then the long long withdrawal, at 2 millimeters a year, the continents separating as a new ocean divides them once more. This entire event of passion, from the moment of initial shy contact — 2 millimeters a year! — to post-coital afterglow is 100 million years in duration. Ruth, he says, let's practice long long withdrawal!

I tell him that the metaphor of amorous contact expresses only the force of a desire — his, not mine. I was just playing, I say. Because I remain content with the truth of rocks as they are. He flips through the pages of the book, stopping at the picture of a huge boulder, the size of a small building, resting perilously at the edge of a mountain top. The boulder has a somewhat darkish cast. The bedrock upon which it rests, and the surrounding rock, does not. He says, Oh, I like that, I like it very much. What he likes so very much is the caption that describes and defines the huge boulder as a glacial erratic. It's the phrase, of course, not what the phrase refers to, that he likes.

Our bodies are wet from head to toe. The yellowing pages of the book that he holds are dampened, and scented, by his touch — by the fingers that have been all over me, and in me. He reads: "A rock transported by glacial ice and deposited at some distance, often great distance, from its geological origin, and resting now on bedrock of alien lithology." Lithology? The study and description of rocks? Yes, I reply, but here meaning the physical character of rocks. The glacial erratic doesn't belong. It's home lies several hundred miles to the north. A footnote informs him of what he, my paramour of the Oxford English Dictionary, already knows. That erratic is from the Latin meaning to wander, prone to wander. He reads the final words of the caption: "Alternatively: lonely erratic." He grins. He says, "You're my glacial erotic."

I don't remind him that the erratic was carried by the glacier. Passive voice. That it didn't wander ("like a nomad," his idea). That although it sits alone in an alien landscape, it is not lonely. That it doesn't know it's far from home.

My husband only says, Just like us, Ruth, reclusive in the Adirondacks — far from home. Two deviants from the standard — erratic together. Geology, he says, is good.

FROM THE MUSIC OF THE INFERNO (1999)

"LAMENT OF AN ESCAPE ARTIST"

The immigrant groundskeeper — father to a nostalgic writer, long fled — removes the Welcome to Utica signs, because nothing is left but a vast, lush meadow, enclosed by a nine-foot chain-link fence, with coils of razor wire rolling and gleaming along the top rail. The fragile father of the nostalgic writer is too old. Nevertheless, he maintains the meadow vigorously, trimming with fanatic care along the fence and among the broken grave stones, as he jokes saltily to himself, aloud, in his native tongue. Then, one day, he stops. Much questioned by the son (from afar, in letters), he responds with silence, this immigrant face, with no expression, nothing to express. The vast meadow reverts to what it was when the Indians, who knew better, and would not live here, called this valley Mohawk. The chain-links rust, give way, to be smothered in thorny underbrush. The garlicky groundskeeper disappears. Like obscene fingers, upright and galvanized, the posts alone endure: *contra naturam*. Utica was here.

APPENDIX ◆ WRITING FICTION AS AN ITALIAN-AMERICAN?

EDITOR'S NOTE

The following was delivered as the keynote address, April 15, 2010, at the conference "For a Dangerous Pedagogy: A Manifesto for Italian and Italian American Studies," organized and directed by Pellegrino D'Acierno and Stanislao Pugliese, at Hofstra University.

I'm a writer according to the only definition of writer that I've ever assented to: that haunted fool who writes because he must — never having had a choice in the matter, which is probably why I never give a thought to my specific identity as a writer, assuming, as I do, that writer-without-modification is specific enough for me. So here I am, at this grand gathering, speaking to you about the writer (me) as Italian-American, but unable to tell you what it would mean (for me) to write fiction as an Italian-American, because I'm not sure that I *am* an Italian-American, or even what an Italian-American is, and were I confident that I was one, I'm sure that I wouldn't tell you that I write as one because I would never have wanted to write as one — even if I *could* write as one, if it were a choice to do so, which I don't think it is — even for those who are confident that they *do* write as Italian-Americans. I don't want to write as a *male*, either, though I seem to be one. Are you with me? (Am I with me?)

The topic of the writer as Italian-American has gained some academic currency (though not all that much) in an era when it is thought to be the higher moral function of the American university to "celebrate diversity." For "American university" think what the late comedian Flip Wilson called "The Church of What's Happening Now." I've always assumed that my role was not to celebrate, but rather to cultivate critical consciousness in myself and in my students. In the academy as we know it, however, intellectuals with funny last names like mine have taken their place, joyfully, in the line of conformity, as they seek to identify, read, and celebrate their own tradition of literature in America: and, to a point, it's a good thing to identify all those brave women and men with funny last names like mine, who have written fiction and poems and plays. There's a surprising lot of it too, a dimension of American literary history that deserves some recognition, but probably not all that

much in the great scheme of things. Because there are all those other hyphen-
ated writers of different races and ethnicities, not to mention all those repre-
hensible others — you know who they are — those that the hyphenates and
the celebrators of the hyphenates like to excoriate as their oppressors. You
know their names: Emerson, Hawthorne, Melville, James, Eliot. Dead white
males. In other words, the canonical sons of bitches and those even worse
sons and daughters of bitches, their academic defenders, who are suspected
in the academy as we know it of being cultural warriors of the extreme Right.

The thing about all the hyphenate literature that has been uncovered and
muscled into the curriculum is that most of it is not bad but simply of unremarkable quality. (On the other hand, the most of any human endeavor is of
unremarkable quality.) As if I've read it all and could pronounce authoritative
judgment upon it because I know it all, which I do not. Nobody knows it all.
There's too much to know. I was actually thinking of only one tradition of hyphenate writers. My own so-called tradition of Italian-American literature.
I've read a great deal of *that,* but hardly all, if there is such a thing as an iden-
tifiable "all," a totality that would include, for example, the unpublished volumes of the poetry of my paternal grandfather, a trouble-making anarchist
and acquaintance of Carlo Tresca, whose manuscripts (my grandfather's) may
be read in the SUNY, Stony Brook archive.

But let's put aside the question of value, the uncomfortable question of
whether the tradition of so-called Italian-American writers is a tradition of
aesthetic excellence, rather than a tradition of sociological documentation,
conveyed inside the standard realist novel. Let's put that question aside because it's sure to derail me, and you, from the central question: What, exactly,
does it mean to call me an Italian-American writer?

Indulge me briefly as I take a short and familiar autobiographical excur-
sion. My four grandparents were born in the south of Italy in the late nineteenth century, and left, you know why, for America. They, certainly, were
Italians, but when they stepped onto the boat in Naples, at that moment, as
they set foot onto that fateful boat in Naples, they began to be somewhat less
Italian, and when they reached Ellis Island and through all those years spent
here until they died in their late 80s, they become slowly, but inevitably, less
and less Italian. They became the kind of Italian whom those who did not
step onto the boat in Naples would recognize as different, and they, my grandparents, when they visited the old country many years after Ellis Island, felt
their difference from those who did not choose to leave. When the immigrant

met, after many years, those in the extended family who did not immigrate, there was a moment, not so easily repressed, of the mutually felt embarrassment of intra-family loneliness and alienation. From one's own blood. Because the immigrant's blood had been modified in the guts of the American experience. So those Italians, like my grandparents, who left Naples around 1900, became at some point first generation Italian-Americans, even though they spoke virtually no English to their dying day. And their children, the second generation, like my parents born and raised here? I need not spell out the reasons why my parents became estranged from their blood.

One story, permit me just this one, which you may say proves, after all, that I *am* an Italian-American writer, at least on a part time basis: One day, my father, as he told it to me, oldest of his siblings, finds his youngest brother crying on the school steps, refusing to go in. When my father asks, what's wrong, Guerrino, his young sibling responds, "I don't want to be Guerrino no more! I don't like that damn name!" (He had been born during World War I and named in its honor by my witty and often merciless grandfather.) My father, a kind man, says, "You don't have to be Guerrino if you don't want to! From now on you tell the teacher that your name is William! Write William from now on on all your school papers. And with your little friends, call yourself Bill!" When I asked my father, in the last weeks of his life, why he chose William, why Bill, Dad, he said in the 1920s his hero was the greatest of all American tennis players, William Tilden, known as Big Bill Tilden, the Babe Ruth of tennis. So a boy who doesn't want to be named Guerrino, gets to be named William, Bill, for all of his life, because his older brother, then all of eleven years old, a son of immigrants, was in love with a sports star who played the game of wealthy Protestant Americans — a game that he, my father, desperately wanted to play, and did play, he told me, on the bumpy dirt playgrounds of Utica, New York, with a ping pong paddle. A comical-sad tale of the second generation.

Let's consider a distinction. Let's pronounce first generation Italian-American with strong stress on the first word: *ITALIAN*-American. And let's say second generation Italian-American with strong stress on the second word: Italian-AMERICAN. And those of us in generation 3, like me, the so-called Italian-American writer? I certainly felt, and yet feel, deep kinship with my maternal grandparents, who had the job of raising me, because both of my parents worked — my parents who had to leave school after the eighth grade, and you know why, I trust. As applied to me, how shall I pronounce Italian-American? With ever-fainter, retreating vocal emphasis on both terms.

There was a time when I lived inside Utica's large Italian-American enclave — that was many years ago, when all those around me as far as the eye could see had funny last names like mine, when I never met "Americans," as they were called, with the inevitable, tired pun on the word, and when it wasn't until I was eighteen years old that I ever saw a Protestant church or a synagogue; a time when I spoke fluently a dialect that I learned as a child in my grandparents' house — a dialect last spoken 100 years ago by peasants of the South, whom the Tuscans barely deign to recognize as Italian and whose dialect was said to me, by a Florentine, to be not Italian but some more or less incomprehensible other language, almost as incomprehensible as the language spoken in Sicily and heard in Visconti's *La Terra Trema*. I became unfluent when I reached college and graduate school and moved to Los Angeles for my first job. I did not study the language and literature of Italy, but that of Great Britain and America, whose writers, especially Joyce, Pound, Stevens, and Hemingway set my artistic ideals for writing.

My mother assumed and actually gave voice to the thought that I would marry, as she put it, "an Italian girl. And don't you forget," she said. I did not marry one; and I must tell you the unpleasant truth that I was repelled by the idea, which felt to me like an invitation to incest, to various semi-alluring acts of uncleanliness. Oh, there's some Italian in me alright, and how proud I was some two years ago when, in Bologna, where they are kinder than in Florence, a distinguished professor of literature, upon hearing me speak my limited Italian told me (she was in shock, I think) that my tone and rhythm were authentic.

According to the hyphenate consciousness of what is misleadingly called the literary wing of the academy, I am constituted as a writer by the following categories:

1) Italian heritage
2) Male
3) Roman Catholic
4) White
5) Heterosexual
6) Working class origin

I *am* those things, according to the thoroughly sociologized literary academic, who works in The Church of What's Happening Now, and nothing more. To know these facts about me is presumably to know all you need to know about me as writer. I do not blame sociologists for understanding writers in this manner. It's not the sociologists who are the problem — they do what they are trained to do. It's the so-called literary professoriate, which has the audacity to call itself literary after it has embraced sociological canons of understanding, and forgotten, if ever it knew, what sociological canons cannot touch: creativity, imagination, art, mystery — the writer's ability to travel far from home and the self that sociological determinants would lumber him (me) with.

The shame of self-loathing literary academics is that they desire the cachet of the so-called soft social scientists, who in their turn desire to wrap themselves in the mantle of the hard scientists. (Humanists are hard-wired, for the last 200 years, to have inferiority complexes.) The desire is to find ways to explain art and thereby get to objective knowledge about its foundations in order to tell us what art *is, essentially* is. The implied logic goes like this: now that we have listed all of the sociological, biological, psychosocial and psychobiological constituents of the writer (this writer, me, as Italian-American), we have told you all that is possible to tell — all that is rationally valuable and knowable about this writer and his writings as Italian-American. We, the forensic pathologists of art, having thoroughly dissected the corpse of his art, have *explained* him.

The trouble with the academic study of literature and the other arts is that it is taken as normal, as good, that literature and the arts *should* be studied. As objects of study they must, of course, be explained. Once explained, the art of the art is banished from view and the explainers reveal themselves as secret adherents of Scientism, that quaint would-be art-killing religion of the nineteenth century, alive and well in current literary departments of the university, where so-called humanists rush to make themselves over as neuroscientists. Mainly, they parrot the jargon and become the poseurs of neuroscience.

(*Explain*: from the Latin, *to spread out completely*, as on a cold slab in a morgue, where organs are cut out and lain side by side, flat, so much the better to be analyzed: no longer part of a three dimensional living whole.)

Okay. My undeniable Italian heritage — does it, or does it not, qualify me as an Italian-American writer? My definition of the classic Italian-American writer is this: someone like Marie Tomasi, Jo Pagano, or Michael De

Capite, second generation types, insiders, often reluctantly so, writing largely inside narratives of their first generation parents and their parents' uncomfortable children, in the genre of realism, sometimes stretched comically to the surrealist breaking point, as in George Panetta's *We Ride a White Donkey* — Panetta, the Mark Twain plus of Italian-American writing. And the best of them all is Mario Puzo's unfortunately entitled *The Fortunate Pilgrim,* a novel whose artistic force makes it one of the important American novels — never mind the hyphenate genre. Can someone of nonItalian heritage write such inside narratives? Highly unlikely, perhaps, though I put nothing past imagination to make breathtaking leaps, to travel freely, very far from home, as Arthur Miller did in *A View from the Bridge.* I have written inside narratives in *The Edge of Night* and *Johnny Critelli,* my first two attempts at fiction some fifteen years ago, though *The Edge of Night* was misleadingly marketed as nonfiction by Random House. Neither of those books qualify as realistic in form and style, as befits a writer who was swept up in his young manhood not by nineteenth century English and French masters of realism, but by modernist experimenters in poetry and prose fiction.

And here's a curious fact about me as a writer of fiction that may please you: many of my major characters have Italian surnames, even when there is nothing, or very little, about them that would qualify them for a place inside the aforementioned insider's narrative of Italian-American life. I don't choose these names, they choose me, and once I'm chosen, these names (Critelli, Assisi, Tagliaferro, Lucchesi, Del Piero, Morelli) make writing a little easier — perhaps even make it possible. The names exert magical power: once written down, an imaginative world suddenly opens up and I find myself foot loose on a fictional adventure. Perhaps what I've just told you gives you every reason to say that my instincts as a writer are fatally Italian-American: instincts are, of course, what we have no, or little, control over. (I imagine myself in a twelve step program for Italian-American addiction: I'm the object of ridicule, after falling off the wagon for the 116th time.)

What I've told you about Italian surnames doesn't, however, explain other characters, equally important in my work, equally magical for inspiration: O.J. Simpson, Herman Melville, Saddam Hussein, Ludwig Wittgenstein, JFK, T.S. Eliot. Nor does it explain — I am male, I'm told, through and through — how it can come to pass that my last three novels feature women as the central subject of my imagination — three leading female characters who have been described to me as "strong women" by more than one of my female readers. Two of the three are named Ruth Cohen and Jennifer Thornberry, while the third is no Italian-American either but the real thing herself: Claudia Cardinale, whom the Italian media dubbed, in ethnocentric pride, in the 1960s, Claudia *nazionale*. Wait: Claudia? The real Italian thing? Born of Sicilian parents. Strike one. In Tunisia. Strike two. Whose native language was French. Strike three. And who learned Italian well enough to dub herself only by the time of "8½," after she'd made several films. So much for these noxious myths of ethnic purity. If you ask me why I make fictional characters out of well-known people, most of whom are dead, and not Italian-American, I will respond: How else shall I enjoy their company?

The difficulty with the concept of the Italian-American writer is its inescapable implication that a writer's writing is equivalent to a writer's genealogy, when the truth (like genealogy itself) is a thousand times more complicated. How far are we willing to go with this ethnic heritage thing? Wallace Stevens? A Dutch-American poet? F. Scott Fitzgerald, an Irish-American writer who gave us the great Irish-American novel, *The Great Gatsby*? And Herman Melville, that Scottish-Dutch-American mongrel — was he programmed by his ethnic mixture to produce that amazing feat of literary mongrelitude, *Moby-Dick*?

The work of the scholars gathered here to establish, chart, and describe the field of Italian-American writing is moving, noble, long overdue, and deserves to be honored, but let's cease this conscription of Don DeLillo, Jay Parini, and Gilbert Sorrentino for the Italian-American literary brigade of American literature. It does not work and it does not bring honor to your honorable project if we become ethnic cheerleaders for our own side. Let's not become participants in the mindless show dominating American universities.

I'd like to be a writer who is not imprisoned by the sociological and biological determinants so in vogue, the sort of person free to travel far from the sometimes suffocating home of neighborhood, thanks to the faster than the speed of light vehicle at the writer's disposal: the imagination, which knows not the limits of those metaphorical, and ghettoizing, neighborhoods of gender, race, ethnicity, or sexual identity.

My grandparents, in economic slavery, left Italy for the freedom of America, where they and their children spent their lives in the Italian-American enclave of Utica, New York. I am making a similar journey: I left Utica, New York, and its Italian-American enclave, for the freedom of America. I have yet to arrive. Where is this place, anyway, that they call America?

The last word belongs to my mother, who was not thinking of physical mechanics when, several times over the course of her life, she looked at me in astonishment, or maybe it was awe, or was it horror? and said: "How did we make you?"

I *am* an Italian-American writer — and I am *not*.

VIA FOLIOS
A refereed book series dedicated to the culture of Italian Americans in North America.

RICHARD VETERE, *The Other Colors in a Snow Storm,* Vol. 77, Poetry, $10

GARIBALDI LAPOLLA, *Fire in the Flesh,* Vol. 76, Fiction & Criticism, $25

GEORGE GUIDA, *The Pope Stories,* Vol. 75, Prose, $15

ROBERT VISCUSI, *Ellis Island,* Vol. 74, Poetry, $28

ELENA GIANINI BELOTTI, *The Bitter Taste of Strangers Bread,* Vol. 73, Fiction, $24

PINO APRILE, *Terroni: All That Has Been Done to Ensure That the Italians of the South Become "Southerners,"* Vol. 72, Ethnic/Cultural Studies, $20

EMANUEL DI PASQUALE, *Harvest,* Vol. 71, Poetry, $10

ROBERT ZWEIG, *Return to Naples,* Vol. 70, Memoir, $16

LETIZIA AIROS AND OTTORINO CAPELLI, EDS., *Guido,* Vol. 69, Italian/American Studies, $12

FRED GARAPHÉ, *Moustche Pete Is Dead! Evviva Baffo Pietro! The* Fra Noi *Columns 1985–19855,* Vol. 67, Literature/Oral History, $12

PAOLO RUFFILLI, *Dark Room,* Vol. 66, Poetry, $10

HELEN BAROLINI, *Crossing the Alps,* Vol. 65, Fiction, $14

COSMO FERRARA, *Profiles of Italian Americans,* Vol. 64, Italian/American Studies, $16

GIL FAGIANI, *Chianti in Connecticut,* Vol. 63, Poetry, $10

PIERO BASSETTI, NICCOLÓ D'AQUINO, *Italic Lessons,* Vol. 62, Italian/American Studies $10

GRACE CAVALIERI AND SABINE PASCARELLI, EDS., *The Poet's Cookbook,* Vol. 61, Poetry/Recipes, $12

EMANUEL DI PASQUALE, *Siciliana,* Vol. 60, Poetry, $8

NATALIA COSTA-ZALESSOW, ED., JOAN E. BORRELLI, TRANSLATOR, *Francesca Turini Bufalini: Autobiographical Poems,* Vol. 59, Poetry, $18

RICHARD VETERE, *Baroque,* Vol. 58, Fiction, $18

LEWIS PUTNAM TURCO, *La Famiglia / The Family,* Vol. 57, Memoir, $15

NICK JAMES MILETI, *The Unscrupulous: Scams, Cons, Fakes, and Fraud That Poison the Fine Arts,* Vol. 56, Humanities, $20

PIERO BASSETTI, PAOLINO ACCOLLA, NICCOLO D'AQUINO, *Italici: An Encounter with Bassetti,* Vol. 55, Italian Studies, $8

GIOSE RIMANELLI, *The Three-Legged One,* Vol. 54, Fiction, $15

CHARLES KLOPP, *Bele Antiche Storie,* Vol. 53, Critiscism, $25

JOSEPH RICAPITO, *Second Wave,* Vol. 52, Poetry, $12

GARY R. MORMINO, *Italians in Florida,* Vol. 51, Italiana Americana/History, $15

GIANFRANCO ANGELUCCI, GIUSEPPE NATALE, TRANSLATOR, *Federico F,* Vol. 50, Fiction, $16

ANTHONY VALERIO, *The Little Sailor,* Vol. 49, Fiction, $8. **OUT OF PRINT**

ROSS TALARICO, *The Reptilian Interludes,* Vol. 48, Poetry, $15

RACHAEL GUIDO DEVRIES, *Teeny Tiny Tino's Fishing Story,* Vol. 47, Children's Literature, $6

VIA FOLIOS
A refereed book series dedicated to the culture of Italian Americans in North America.

EMANUEL DI PASQUALE, *Writing Anew: New and Selected Poems,* Vol. 46, Poetry, $15

MARIA FAMA, *Looking for Cover,* Vol. 45, Poetry, $15

ANTHONY VALERIO, *Toni Cade Bambara's One Sicilian Night,* Vol. 44, Memoir, $44.
OUT OF PRINT

EMANUEL CARNEVALI, DENNIS BARONE, ED., *Furnished Rooms,* Vol. 43, Poetry, $14

GEORGE GUIDA, *Low Italian,* Vol. 41, Poetry, $10

GARDAPHE, GIORDANO, TAMBURRI, *Introducing Italian Americana: Generalities on Literature and Film, a bilingual forum,* Vol. 40, Italian/American Studies, $10

DANIELA GIOSEFFI, *Blood Autumn/Autunno di sangue,* Vol. 39, Poetry, $15/$25

FRED MISURELLA, *Lies to Live by,* Vol. 38, Stories, $15

STEVEN BELLUSCIO, *Constructing a Bibliography,* Vol. 37, Italian Americana, $15

ANTHONY J. TAMBURRI, ed., *Italian Cultural Studies 2002,* Vol. 36, Essays, $18

BEA TUSIANI, *con amore,* Vol. 35, Memoir, $19

FLAVIA BRIZIO-SKOV, ed., *Reconstructing Societies in the Aftermath of War,*
   Vol. 34, History, $30

TAMBURRI, ET AL, eds., *Italian Cultural Studies 2001,* Vol. 33, Essays, $18

ELIZABETH G. MESSINA, ed., *In Our Own Voices,* Vol. 32, Italian American Studies, $25

STANISLAO G. PUGLIESE, *Desperate Inscriptions,* Vol. 31, History, $12

HOSTERT & TAMBURRI, eds., *Screening Ethnicity,* Vol. 30, Italian American Culture, $25

G. PARATI & B. LAWTON, eds., *Italian Cultural Studies,* Vol. 29, Essays, $18

HELEN BAROLINI, *More Italian Hours,* Vol. 28, Fiction, $16

FRANCO NASI, ed., *Intorno alla Via Emilia,* Vol. 27, Culture, $16

ARTHUR L. CLEMENTS, *The Book of Madness & Love,* Vol. 26, Poetry, $10

JOHN CASEY, ET AL., *Imagining Humanity,* Vol. 25, Interdisciplinary Studies, $18

ROBERT LIMA, *Sardinia/Sardegna,* Vol. 24, Poetry, $10

DANIELA GIOSEFFI, *Going On,* Vol. 23, Poetry, $10

ROSS TALARICO, *The Journey Home,* Vol. 22, Poetry, $12

EMANUEL DI PASQUALE, *The Silver Lake Love Poems,* Vol. 21, Poetry, $7

JOSEPH TUSIANI, *Ethnicity,* Vol. 20, Poetry, $12

JENNIFER LAGIER, *Second-Class Citizen,* Vol. 19, Poetry, $8

FELIX STEFANILE, *The Country of Absence,* Vol. 18, Poetry, $9

PHILIP CANNISTRARO, *Blackshirts,* Vol. 17, History, $12

LUIGI RUSTICHELLI, ed., *Seminario sul racconto,* Vol. 16, Narrative, $10

LEWIS TURCO, *Shaking the Family Tree,* Vol. 15, Memoirs, $9

LUIGI RUSTICHELLI, ed., *Seminario sulla drammaturgia,* Vol. 14, Theater/Essays, $10

FRED GARDAPHÈ, *Moustache Pete Is Dead! Long Live Moustache Pete!*
   Vol. 13, Oral Lit., $10

JONE GAILLARD CORSI, *Il libretto d'autore, 1860–1930,* Vol. 12, Criticism, $17

HELEN BAROLINI, *Chiaroscuro: Essays of Identity,* Vol. 11, Essays, $15